THE LETTER KILLETH

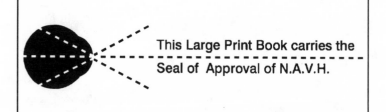

This Large Print Book carries the
Seal of Approval of N.A.V.H.

THE LETTER KILLETH

RALPH MCINERNY

THORNDIKE PRESS
An imprint of Thomson Gale, a part of The Thomson Corporation

Detroit • New York • San Francisco • New Haven, Conn. • Waterville, Maine • London

THOMSON

GALE

LIBRARY OF CONGRESS CATALOGING-IN-PUBLICATION DATA

McInerny, Ralph M.
    The letter killeth / by Ralph McInerny.
      p. cm. — (Thorndike Press large print basic)
    ISBN-13: 978-0-7862-9393-3 (alk. paper)
    ISBN-10: 0-7862-9393-4 (alk. paper)
    1. Knight, Roger (Fictitious character) — Fiction. 2. Knight, Philip (Fictitious character) — Fiction. 3. Private investigators — Indiana — South Bend — Fiction. 4. Mail bombings — Fiction. 5. University of Notre Dame — Fiction. 6. College teachers — Fiction. 7. Large type books. 8. College stories.
    I. Title.
    PS3563.A31166L48 2007
    813'.54—dc22   2006101183

Published in 2007 by arrangement with St. Martin's Press, LLC.

Printed in the United States of America on permanent paper
10 9 8 7 6 5 4 3 2 1

For Bill Miscamble, C.S.C.

PART ONE

1

Winter lingers in northern Indiana, and snow continues to fall well into March, courtesy of Lake Michigan. Sometimes, of course, snow comes fluttering down with all the sweetness of a Christmas card, the weather almost balmy, puffs of breath before the face a delightful joke. More often than not, however, the temperature hovers around zero, and snow comes in on a blast of frigid wind that sends students scurrying across the campus from room to library to class to dining hall, all bundled up like Nanook of the North. Fortunately the campus walks are quickly cleared or it would have been impossible for Roger Knight to get around in his golf cart. For his brother, Phil, the Notre Dame winters were the only blemish in their current life. Not even following the fortunes of the hockey team could keep Florida from his mind as the days grew short and overcast and the snow deeper.

"You should go, Phil," Roger urged.

"But you can't get away now."

"What does that have to do with it? Phil, you know I don't golf or play tennis." Roger paused. "Of course, you smile. The thought is ridiculous. Check with the travel bureau."

"Maybe I will."

Later, Roger got on the Web and went to a travel site and looked into plane tickets and resorts in the Sarasota area. Of course, he could not make the arrangements final without Phil's go-ahead.

"You're trying to get rid of me."

"Of course, if you insist, I could resign from the faculty and go off with you."

"Ha. Actually, I'm beginning to like this kind of winter."

"Snow eventually melts, Phil."

Yes, and the sun also rises, but it would have been difficult to prove that in the gray and overcast days that lay ahead. How much gloomier it would have been without the snow.

Phil's decision to stay was not the result of anything Roger said. It was the letters.

Father Carmody called and told Phil, "You'll think I'm crazy."

"The weather getting to you, Father?"

"What's wrong with the weather?"

"Have you been out lately?"

"I am just this minute leaving the Main Building. I think I've taken on a fool's errand, and I want company. Can I come over there?"

"I could come to Holy Cross House."

"It'll be easier for me to come there."

Father Carmody was a reluctant resident of Holy Cross House, not because he did not like the accommodations of the retirement home for priests, but because of its associations. All the other residents save one or two were sliding slowly from this life, often having already left their minds behind. Father Carmody had his meals in his room so as to avoid the refectory where old men were spoon-fed by nurses, their chins wiped, all the while being talked to as if they were babies. Many of the most pathetic cases were men years younger than Father Carmody.

Father Wangle had given him excellent advice when he moved in. "Avoid all gatherings, refuse to take part in physical therapy, get your hair cut on campus."

The reason for the last remark became clear to Father Carmody when he saw the wheelchairs lined up, their occupants, many once prominent and powerful in the congre-

11

gation or in the university, awaiting their turn to get a haircut that would have done a marine recruit proud.

"Stay active," Wangle said, summing it up.

Father Carmody had stayed active, perhaps too active for some. There were times when he felt like the Ghost of Christmas Past when he dropped in on the president or provost to give them the advantage of his thoughts on this or that. Once he had been a powerful presence in the university administration, not out front, but influencing the course of things from discreet obscurity. Officers came and went, golden boys rose and fell, but Father Carmody had always survived, ready to guide neophytes along the paths of effective administration.

Nowadays he did not speak softly, but he carried no big stick. In the provost's outer office, he took a chair and fell into conversation with a young priest he did not know. How pink and blond he looked. And nervous. Ah well, coming to see the provost was like a visit to Oz. Father Carmody sought to cheer him up, asked his name, found that he had studied in Rome.

"Ah, Rome."

"Have you been there, Father?"

Carmody looked sharply at the young

priest, but neither humor nor insolence seemed to explain the preposterous question. No point in explaining that he had been in Rome as assistant general of the Congregation of Holy Cross during what he liked to think were the boom years. Obviously Father Conway did not recognize him. Well, for that matter, ten minutes had passed before he realized that Conway was an assistant provost.

"I'm thinking of visiting," Father Carmody murmured.

"We have a house there, you know."

This is what it will be like after I am dead, Father Carmody thought. Like grass of the field, swept away to be burnt, and no memory of it left. He had become a stranger in the institution to which he had devoted the long years of his life. Well, what did he want, a life-sized statue like those of Ned and Ted in front of the library? His name on a building or two? Better try to wring spiritual benefit from it. We have here no lasting city. Heaven's my destination.

The young priest was Tim Conway, and he had only recently been appointed assistant to the provost.

"And what are your tasks?"

"Troubleshooting. Mostly student affairs so far."

"Isn't there a prefect of student affairs?"

"You must mean Iglesias."

Father Carmody frowned. "The singer?"

Tim looked blank. "No, Ben Iglesias. Student affairs."

"He's the prefect?"

"He's a vice president."

"Of course."

What Father Carmody thought of the bureaucratization of the university and the resulting multiplication of administrative officers was a subject best brought up during a visit to the community cemetery, where he could walk the rows of identical crosses, communing with the dead and letting them know what Charles Carmody thought of what was going on around here.

Just then the provost emerged from his office and cried out, "Father Carmody! I thought I heard your voice."

Much shaking of hands, smiles all around, and did Father Conway realize who he had been talking to? In short, a great fuss was made over the unexpected visit of the old priest who had advised presidents since the early days of the Hesburgh regime. Carmody was beginning to think that being forgotten was preferable to this kind of attention.

"I was just going to tell Father Carmody about those letters," Father Conway said with a touch of obsequiousness.

The provost's eyebrows shot up and his eyes rounded, though his smile did not falter. "Let's go into my office, shall we?"

There, in a comfortable island of furniture in a corner of the vast inner room, they sat. Father Carmody refused coffee. The provost composed himself and began.

It was, he was sure, a tempest in a teapot. With a little laugh, he took an envelope from his inner pocket and handed it to the old priest. The message was in block letters, some capitals, some not. BeWarE! yOUr ofFice WilL bE bomBEd. GOD is nOt moCked. The letters had been Scotch-taped to a sheet of paper.

Father Carmody read it a second time. "How did you get this?"

"My secretary found it slipped under the door when she arrived yesterday morning."

"Some student's idea of a joke."

"Of course." But the provost sounded dubious. "Others have received similar letters."

The dean of Arts and Letters. The football coach.

"The football coach?"

It was difficult to think that any student

15

could be otherwise than elated by the abrupt reversal in the fortunes of the Fighting Irish wrought by Charlie Weis. That certain members of the administration or of the faculty might have their lives brightened by a bomb in their office seemed a pardonable student fantasy. To threaten to blow up the Guglielmino Center was something very much else.

"This is the sort of thing you always handled," the provost said.

"I'll take this." Father Carmody folded the sheet and stuffed it into a pocket.

"What will you do?"

"I'll ask Phil Knight for help."

The provost had to think. "The brother of Professor Knight."

"He is a licensed private detective. For that matter, so is Roger."

"Roger Knight is a detective?"

"Was. Before we brought him here as the Huneker Professor of Catholic Studies. His brother came with him. He is more or less inactive now, but he has been of help to the university on a number of occasions."

"We don't want any publicity."

"If we did, we would call in the South Bend police."

"Not even Notre Dame security knows of

16

these letters."

"I should hope not."

The provost came with Father Carmody into the reception area, where a man rose from his seat, a look of expectation on his face. The provost blanched.

"Mr. Quirk."

Quirk hurried to Father Carmody and put out his hand. "Quirk, Ned. Class of '65. I'll bet you don't remember me."

Carmody smiled. "You lived in Dillon. You're from Kansas City and majored in electrical engineering."

"Civil."

"You changed your major?"

The provost threw up his hands in delight. "Father Carmody, you are remarkable!"

"The place was smaller then." He couldn't resist adding, "Once we didn't even have a provost. Only an academic vice president."

Quirk, smallish and rotund, bald as an egg, beamed. "I don't recognize the campus anymore."

Then, as it sometimes will to any administrator, an idea came to the provost. "Ned, why don't you discuss your suggestion with Father Carmody? I would be seeking his advice in any case."

This was a diplomatic bum's rush, of

course, but Father Carmody fell in with the plan. He took Quirk's arm, and they went into the hall.

"What did they do to this building, Father?" Quirk looked around him with dismay.

"For the most part, simply restored it to its original condition. Not these grand offices, of course. Come."

In the elevator, he asked Quirk what he had wanted to talk to the provost about.

"Does the name F. Marion Crawford mean anything to you?"

"Is the pope German? Come on. We're going to visit the Knight brothers."

2

Beauty lies, not in the eye of the beholder nor in the mere thereness of the beheld, but in some complicated relation between the two. In fact, the beloved thing itself, or the person herself, is seldom seen at all, if seeing lies in mere perception. What wife ever sees her husband as does some neutral observer, if such there be? What husband who might say of the wife of his bosom that she walks in beauty like the night imagines that he is describing her for all to see? Third parties are notoriously mystified by what draws this man to this woman. They may have eyes to see but are unable to see what for the smitten is all in all.

Such thoughts and their expression characterized the discussion of the University Club of Notre Dame as the members sought to deal with the news that the dear squat building, the dining room with its vaulted roof, and the poky backroom bar, where the discussions went on, were all doomed to destruction. An edict had gone out from the Main Building announcing that the club would be razed to make way for an extension of Engineering, and the outraged members of the club were thrust into the position of one whose spouse is spoken of by a stranger.

In the dining room, at the facetiously named Algonquin table, in a corner where the self-described Old Bastards met for lunch, and at other tables where more random diners congregated, the sense that a Sword of Damocles hung over this familiar setting provided the common subject of the day. There is a music of anger, largely percussive and profane, and the club had swelled with it ever since the judgment had been circulated to the members.

The administrator with the hyphenated name was subjected to imaginative abuse.

"Who is he?" demanded Potts, professor emeritus of philosophy, surveying the other OBs with a rheumy eye.

"What do you mean, who is he?" Wheeler barked, as if his anger could be directed at Potts.

"I mean I never heard of him. How long has he been here?"

Potts had celebrated the golden anniversary of his joining the faculty, and anyone with less than a quarter of a century on campus had for him the status of an unregistered alien. Someone guessed, and Potts snorted.

"I knew Montana," Armitage Shanks said.

"The quarterback?"

"The architect. Frank Montana. He designed this building."

"Is he to blame for the acoustics?"

How sweetly sad it was to think that once complaints about the acoustics in the dining room might have provided topic enough to get them through a meal.

"Speak well of the dead," Shanks advised. "There's nothing wrong with the acoustics. It's your hearing that is defective."

"What?"

"Can he be stopped?"

"Who?"

"The man you don't know. The man who has no sense of the tradition of this place. He thinks it is just a building that can be torn down and replaced with another."

"It can be and it will be." Bingham, late of the law school, spoke with the mordant satisfaction of a magistrate invoking the death penalty. "We have been put in the position of those poor widows who learn that a new highway will be run through their living room. Eminent domain. Protests are useless."

A special meeting of the membership had been called, a committee formed, and an elaborate report prepared and sent to the Main Building. Its only result had been a statement that a new place might possibly be found for the club. Perhaps a donor could be found . . .

"A donor gave the money for this building!" Potts cried.

The Gore family had financed the building of the club with the understanding that a massive collection of beer steins would be housed there. And so they were, enshrined in a number of glass cases in the wall that separated the sunken dining room from a series of all-purpose rooms on a higher level.

"Have they been told?" Bingham asked.

"The original donor is dead."

"His family, then?"

"They are not pleased."

"They should be furious. Is there a statute of limitations on the recognition of benefactions?"

All looked to Bingham. He shrugged. "If they want to tear this place down, nothing can stop them."

"It'll be the Grotto next. Or Sacred Heart Basilica."

"The Main Building could simply be burned. That's a tradition."

The predecessor of the Main Building had gone up in flames in 1879 and within a year been replaced by the present edifice. Father Sorin, the founder of the university, had been away from campus when the terrible news came to him, and he returned immediately, vowing to rebuild within a year, and so he had.

"Where is Sorin now?" Potts asked piously.

"The question is theological."

"In the community cemetery."

Plaisance sighed. "It is enough to make one half in love with easeful death."

"Nothing lasts."

"The place has fallen into the hands of barbarians."

On and on went the discussion, engaged in with the peculiar satisfaction that morose delectation provides. Plaisance had come as near as any of them to the admission that this latest outrage promised to provide the subject of discussion for many future meals at the Old Bastards' table.

"We should march on the Main Building in protest."

"We could let our hair grow, and our beards. Only the unruly get a hearing."

"Not even God could grow your hair, Potts."

"What?"

They were interrupted by Debbie, the hostess, offering more coffee. The thought of consuming more liquid caused unease, as she knew it would. They looked around and noticed as if with surprise that they were the last occupants of the dining room.

"We're going, we're going."

"Watch your language."

3

Bill Fenster's grandfather had made a fortune during World War II as a defense contractor, although to his dying day he described the conflict as Mr. Roosevelt's war. With the coming of peace, he had sold off everything and invested so wisely and widely that he had provided for his progeny into the second and third generation, and doubtless far beyond. In the postwar period, Grandpa Fenster had lent his support to the John Birch Society and to the campaign to get the United States out of the UN and the UN out of the United States. Bill's father, perhaps in reaction, had drifted leftward and worked for the doomed Gene McCarthy campaign. McCarthy's defeat and the later debacle of George McGovern had cured Bill's father of politics and provided his grandfather with satisfaction at this proof of his son's naïveté. The son, Manfred, called Fred, had then turned to religion and spent much of the year traveling to reported new apparitions of the Blessed Virgin. When Bill was accepted at Notre Dame, his father had attributed this to the intercession of the Blessed Virgin, whereas his grandfather was certain that in his generosity to the university lay the explanation. Thank God he hadn't put the family name on any buildings.

"Don't make my mistake," his father advised Bill.

"How so?"

"I never had to earn my living. Neither will you. I have come to think that money is a curse."

"You could disinherit me."

"Not even your grandfather could have done that. I'm afraid you're doomed to affluence. I have found that the best way is to live as if one were poor."

Bill's mother had died when he was four, worn out after a series of miscarriages when she was trying desperately to provide a brother or sister for him.

"Actually, she had dreamed of a huge family. Eight, nine, even more."

His father had never remarried. It was surprising he hadn't entered a monastery. He spent a week every year with the Trappists in Gethsemani, Kentucky. Bill had joined him there for a few days, once.

"It's not what it was," his father said afterward.

Bill said nothing. He had found it unnerving to be off in the woods like that, life on the farm, sort of, except for the services in church when the high-pitched keening voices rose to where he and his father knelt in the visitors' loft in the middle of the night. They could have used a second bass or two. It turned out that his father thought the life was not austere enough.

"It was like marine boot camp when I first went there. Their heads were shaved, total silence, no Muzak in the guests' refectory."

His father mimicked the life of a poor man and was half a priest himself, saying the office in Latin every day. It was from one of the readings in Advent that his father had typed out a text from Isaiah for Bill to translate when he had been in prep school: "Et aures tuae audient verbum post tergum monentis: 'Haec est via, ambulate in ea, et non declinetis neque ad dexteram neque ad sinistram.' " It had become Bill's motto and hung framed over his desk at Notre Dame.

"What's it mean?" Hogan, his roommate, asked.

"I thought you took Latin."

"In high school."

27

"It says, 'Your ears will hear a voice behind you warning: This is the way, walk in it, and do not turn either to right or left.' "

It wasn't political advice, of course, but Bill took it that way, too, determined to avoid the opposite extremes his grandfather and father had embraced. But he had accepted his father's advice about keeping secret that he already had the wealth most of his classmates dreamed of acquiring. He himself had financed the alternative campus paper he and Mary Alice and Hogan and some others had started. The *Via Media.*

"The donor prefers to remain anonymous," he said, which was true enough.

They put the quote from Isaiah on the masthead, in Latin. Recent issues had been concerned with the fate of the University Club, suggesting that the decision to tear it down and replace it was not only autocratic but indicative of a worrisome trend toward running Notre Dame as if it were a business. "The Bottom Line" was a regular feature in the irregularly appearing newspaper, chronicling the salaries of administrators and coaches, the swollen endowment that was never used to bring down the cost of a Notre Dame education to students. Nothing strident, just the chiding voice of reason. Bill had become a bit of an amateur in the history of the university. Sometimes he reminded himself of his father lamenting what had happened to the Trappists.

His father's visits to the campus were always unannounced. He would call from the Morris Inn and ask Bill to have lunch with him there. Today Bill found his father seated in the lobby. He rose and shuffled toward his son. Worn corduroy pants, baggy cable-knit sweater, tousled hair almost all gray now, he really looked like the poor man that he had wanted to let out of the very rich man he was.

"It was spur of the moment," he said unnecessarily, when they had been shown to their table near a window that looked out on the snowy world. "I forgot how cold it is here in February."

"There's not much going on."

"I want to look into the Catholic Worker House in town. Have you ever been there?"

"What is it?"

"Dorothy Day. Surely you've heard of her."

"Notre Dame gave her the Laetare Medal."

"That's hardly her claim to fame. Not that fame is what she wanted."

So Bill got an account of Dorothy Day and Peter Maurin and the Catholic Worker movement that still went on years after the deaths of its saintly founders.

"I ran into a classmate of mine," his father said, changing the subject. "It's the risk you run."

His father never returned for alumni reunions; he never came for football games. Yet he was a proud if critical alumnus. Bill had not told his father of founding *Via Media*. He hadn't told him of Mary Alice either.

"A fellow named Quirk. Why he remembered me, I don't know. It's even more surprising that I remembered him."

4

Mary Alice Frangipani was the eldest of six Frangipanis, a native of Morristown, New Jersey, where her father was senior partner in the law firm that bore his name. He had graduated from Seton Hall, but his unfulfilled dream had been to go to Notre Dame, and sometimes Mary Alice felt she was living out his dream. He called every other day, avid for a blow-by-blow account of her life on the campus that was for him the earthly paradise. He attended every Notre Dame football game, at home and away, but Mary Alice did not find his passion for athletics contagious. Her father was wild about Charlie Weis.

"Do you know what they're paying him?"

"He's worth every nickel of it whatever it is."

"It started at two million dollars. Who knows what it is now?"

The whole family had attended the Fiesta

Bowl on January 2, flying out in her father's Learjet. Her father had been in ecstasy. He attributed the outcome to bigoted officials. You would have thought they were all obtaining a plenary indulgence for cheering on the Fighting Irish.

Her major had been English until, in disgust, she had switched to the Program of Liberal Studies. Her father had thought English was a quixotic major, but the switch baffled him even more.

"What can you do with it?"

"Nothing."

"You better marry a rich man."

She thought vaguely of graduate school, maybe philosophy. If that thought was vague, anything beyond was vaguer still. Did she want to be a professor? The one professor she unequivocally admired was Roger Knight, and he was anything but typical. It was in one of Knight's classes that she had met Bill Fenster. They were taking another this semester, devoted to F. Marion Crawford. Neither of them had admitted that they didn't have the faintest idea who F. Marion Crawford was. Roger Knight could make a class on Edgar Rice Burroughs exciting. She had told him as much.

"Of course you couldn't connect him to Notre Dame."

"You're wrong, you know. When he was a student at what was called Michigan College he managed to schedule a game with Notre Dame."

"How do you know these things?"

"Constant attention to trivia. You know the name for the first three of the seven liberal arts?"

Why did such tangential things seem the very reason one wanted a higher education? When he first heard Bill's name, he had said, "Ah, window."

"Just don't defenestrate me."

"I'll spare you the pane."

Mary Alice hadn't followed that, but Bill explained it to her later. "I'm surprised he didn't comment on your name."

They both loved Roger Knight and seemed to be his favorites. After the first class of his they had attended, they came outside with him to his golf cart to find that the battery was dead. Bill plugged it in, and while it recharged he amused them by asking why the Battery in New York was called that. And why are the pitcher and catcher called a battery? How quickly the battery recharged, but they walked beside him as he drove to the apartment he shared with his brother, Philip.

"What does he do?"

"He's a private detective."

"Come on."

"It's true. And so am I. Or was. My being offered a chair here changed our lives."

He asked them in, but they were shy, thinking he was just being polite. Eventually, though, they did come to know him in his now native habitat. The whole apartment seemed a study, books everywhere, but also a giant television before which Phil was often sprawled in a beanbag chair watching some game or another. Mary Alice's father would have liked Phil. She didn't want to think what he would make of Roger Knight.

"Crawford was born in Rome, son of the sculptor who made the figure of Liberty atop the Capitol in Washington. His aunt was Julia Ward Howe. Although he was raised in Rome, he didn't become a Catholic until he went to India as a journalist. His first novel was based on his experience there. He lectured at Notre Dame in 1897."

That is how the class on F. Marion Crawford began. Roger Knight's courses always related, one way or another, to the past of Notre Dame, and this was no exception, although there had only been that one visit to the campus by the author who in his day had known a popularity that was the envy of Henry James. Roger began with a discussion of *With the Immortals.*

"An unusual novel, not really a novel at all, but a sort of philosophical dialogue. I have always thought that the figure of Samuel Johnson is the most successful. We will be considering Crawford's theory of fiction later."

Mary Alice had written a profile of Roger Knight for *Via Media.* It gave her a chance to quiz him about his past. It turned out to be even more exotic than she had imagined. He and his older brother had been orphaned, but Phil had been old enough to keep them together and raise Roger. Had Roger always been so fat?

"I was briefly thin in the navy."

"The navy!"

"I enlisted after I got my doctorate at Princeton."

"In what?"

"They called it philosophy."

He had still been a teenager when he got his Ph.D. His age and his avoirdupois had made getting a teaching position difficult, and rather than subsist on postdoctoral fellowships, he had slimmed down enough to join the navy. Meanwhile, Phil had become a very successful private investigator. After Roger's discharge from the navy they settled in Rye, New York. Roger, too, got a private investigator's license, and they had accepted only cases of unusual interest. Their undemanding life had enabled Roger to pursue the life of the mind, and via the Internet he was in contact with kindred spirits around the globe. It was his monograph on Baron Corvo and its surprising popularity that had brought him to the attention of Father Carmody, who nominated Roger for the Huneker Chair in Catholic Studies, the funding for which Carmody had secured from a Philadelphia alumnus.

"Who is Baron Corvo?" Mary Alice asked.

"Was. His real name was Frederick Rolfe." And he told her a thing or two about the disenchanted convert to Catholicism.

"You should give a course on him."

"I have."

"I suppose you've given one on Huneker, too."

"Not yet."

Several agnostic courses in graduate school had been the prelude to Roger's own conversion to Catholicism. "Philosophy has been called the formulation of bad arguments for what you already believe. That is certainly true of disbelief."

"My father is here," Bill told Mary Alice

after Roger's class today.

"In this weather? What's going on?"

"He came on impulse. He usually does."

She waited. Would he want her to meet his father? He seemed to be asking himself the same question.

"You could have dinner with us tonight. At the Morris Inn."

"Should I dress up?"

He laughed. "Wait until you meet my father."

5

When Father Carmody arrived with Quirk in tow, he displayed the letter the provost had received. Phil levered himself out of his beanbag chair and took the letter from Roger.

"A joke?"

"Who knows? Several other administrators and one faculty member received similar notes, apparently. I haven't seen them. Another went to Charlie Weis."

"Weis!"

Quirk seemed indifferent to Father Carmody's mission. He stood, smiling at Roger and shaking his head.

"Is it true?"

"That depends on what you mean by 'it.'"

"You're interested in F. Marion Crawford?"

"I am giving a course on him this semester."

"You are! That's wonderful. I never even

heard his name when I was a student here."

Father Carmody rolled his eyes and took Phil into the study.

"Have you ever been to the Villa Crawford in Sorrento?" Quirk asked Roger.

"You have."

"Several times. I have a great idea. Father Carmody tells me you are just the one to propose it to the administration."

"I think he's pulling your leg."

Quirk ignored this. When he had entered, he had thrown back the hood of his parka, a commodious jacket with NOTRE DAME SWIMMING emblazoned on it. Roger commented on this.

"I was on the swimming team. Of course, there was only the pool in Rockne then."

"What is your great idea?"

Quirk rubbed his head as if to verify that it was hairless. He had not stopped smiling since he came in. Now he grew serious. Roger was aware of the many countries in which Notre Dame students could spend a year abroad. St. Mary's has a Rome program, and so does Architecture. What was needed was a place with associations with Notre Dame.

"Notre Dame as it was. Notre Dame as it should be."

"Is the villa for sale?"

"Everything is for sale."

"Isn't it a convent?"

Quirk tapped the tip of his nose. "I have reason to think that Notre Dame could buy the place."

"Villa Quirk?"

"What do you mean?"

"Most donors like their name given to the buildings they provide the university."

"Oh no no no. Good Lord, I don't have that kind of money."

"What kind of money would be involved?"

"Euros." His eyes widened and he laughed. "You mean, how much? Like everything, that is negotiable."

Roger was beginning to realize that Father Carmody had palmed this enthusiast off on him. Despite Quirk's easy confidence that the villa Crawford had built in Sorrento on the princely proceeds of his fiction could be bought, Roger did not get the impression that Quirk was a practical man. The way he spoke of the purchasability of whatever one might covet and his vagueness as to what sum would be needed if his improbable scheme were adopted did not suggest a man at home in the rough-and-tumble world of buying and selling.

By this time, he had got Quirk into a chair and was trying not to glance enviously to where Phil and Father Carmody were huddled in conversation. Roger's curiosity had been aroused by the letter the old priest had brought, and he was almost as struck as Phil had been to hear that such a threat had been made to the football coach as well. Charlie Weis had taken Notre Dame football from the nadir to the peaks in a single year. Already, he was spoken of in the same breath as Knute Rockne, a comparison he of course dismissed. But he was indisputably a national figure, and the news that threats had been made on him, particularly after the Fiesta Bowl debacle, would be broadcast from coast to coast. Quirk, on the other hand, was completely absorbed in his quixotic project. Had he even understood the import of these threatening letters? Given the potential for bad publicity for the university, it was probably just as well Quirk seemed unaware of this.

"So you're an alumnus."

"Do you know that Father Carmody actually remembered me? Incredible. I was not, I can tell you, a campus luminary during my time here."

"And what have you done since graduating?"

"Wondering how I could have been so little interested in Notre Dame during the years I was here. A student's four years on campus are over almost as soon as they begin. You would be surprised how small a part of a student's interest is engaged in the classes he takes, in learning. Before you know it, you graduate and get swept up in life. Gradually it dawns on you that you all but wasted the opportunity of a lifetime. I have resolved to make up for that."

"Hence your interest in F. Marion Crawford?"

"Yes." He paused. "I collect Notre Dame memorabilia. Books about the place. I have someone who keeps on the lookout for me. She came upon a mention of Notre Dame in a biography of Crawford. You know he lectured here?"

"So did Henry James and William Butler Yeats."

"But they weren't Catholics! Have you read the chapter on Crawford in Louis Auchincloss's *The Man Behind the Book*? I wonder how much of Crawford he actually read. And he doesn't even mention his conversion to Catholicism." Quirk might have pronounced that scandalous sentence in italics.

"You yourself have read Crawford?"

"I have everything but a title or two. There were two complete editions, and he was very popular, so most of the books are easily found. But there are some that are very rare."

"I got my set for a song."

Quirk was on his feet. "Could I see it?"

Roger wished he had brought his chair from his study, the one he could wheel around in without getting to his feet. He rose slowly and with an effort.

"How much do you weigh?" Quirk asked wondrously.

"That depends."

"On what?"

"Whether I can get my brother to read the scale." He patted his rotund circumference. "I can't see it."

Roger waddled into his study, got into the specially built chair that made him mobile, and turned to find that Quirk had stopped in the doorway. His mouth was open as he looked around.

"What a room!"

"That wall is fiction. You will find Crawford there."

Quirk found them, ran his finger along their spines. "The Collier edition."

"The library has a good selection. I couldn't teach the course otherwise."

"He should be reprinted."

"Another costly project. I wonder how

many would be interested in his style of fiction now."

"How can we know if he isn't available?"

"That doesn't sound like a premise any publisher would be willing to proceed on."

"Notre Dame Press should do it."

"Perhaps, with a subsidy . . ." Roger was beginning to feel the beginnings of impatience. He could have tolerated Quirk's enthusiasm if he would not far rather have been talking with Phil and Father Carmody of the threatening letter the priest had brought. Obviously, he wanted Phil to look into the matter.

"You're right, of course. But first things first. I mean the Villa Crawford. As it happens, I do have an idea where the money to buy it could be gotten."

"That wouldn't settle the matter, of course."

"This morning at the Morris Inn — I'm staying there — I ran into a classmate I had not seen in years. He lives a very simple life by the looks of him, and while he was here few people had any inkling of his background. He is rich as Croesus. Inherited money. I had an uncle who worked for his father, that's how I got the story. Manfred swore me to secrecy when I mentioned it to him."

"Manfred?"

"Manfred Fenster."

6

In a dull time, even a small task is welcome. Phil Knight felt that he and Father Carmody were colluding in making a mountain out of a molehill by pretending that the threatening letter the provost had received was anything more than a prank. What made it hard to dismiss was the fact that a similar threat had been made against the football coach.

"You really think there's anything to it, Father?"

"Even as a hoax it could make bad publicity for the university."

"Maybe that's the idea. Just a little rumble in the media."

"That's where you come in, Phil. Those letters have to be collected and their recipients warned against making them known." Father Carmody paused. "How many people already know of them? Someone is sure to say something that will be picked up by the press."

There seemed to be four letters in all:

to the provost
to the dean of Arts & Letters
to the football coach
to Professor Oscar Wack

"Who's he, Roger?"

Roger smiled. "He teaches theory."

"Theory of what?"

"He's in the English department. I think he has joint appointments in theology and law. He is a tireless writer to campus publications. That is odd since he is, as they say, widely published in his field. Cabalistic pieces on various works of literature. I am told he despises me."

"Do you know him?"

"He snubs me. When he sees me coming in my golf cart, he cuts off across the lawn to avoid me. He accuses me of corrupting the young."

"What?"

"I am sure I was his target. It was in a four part series he wrote for the *Observer*. He spoke of unearned and inflated reputations." Roger patted his tummy. "He inveighed against the resurrecting of authors who were enjoying a deep and deserved obscurity. I am told he is less oblique in class, where I am mentioned by name. The dark Knight of the soul, that sort of thing."

"Maybe you pasted together these threats."

"Oh, I did worse. I referred to him in my class as Wack, O. It was taken up by the students."

Phil went first to the Guglielmino Center to find that Weis was on the road recruiting. Father Carmody had prepared the way with a phone call, and an assistant took Phil into his office and handed him the letter.

"I thought the provost ought to know."

"He got one, too."

The man's face brightened. "He did?"

"There were others as well."

"Why do I find that reassuring?"

The letter to Weis had a different message. BewaRe! gOlden boWls brEaK. BoMbs awAy.

"Coach said ignore it. I didn't think so. What do you think?"

"Some nut."

"Some nuts are dangerous." The man looked around. "If anything happened to this place . . ."

"How many people know about this?"

"Here? Only me. And Coach, of course."

48

■ ■ ■ ■

The office of the dean of Arts and Letters was a warren of rooms reached from a posh reception area. Phil was led as through a maze to the inner sanctum where the dean, in shirt sleeves and gaudy suspenders, rose, smiling a crooked smile.

"Phil Knight."

"I know. The provost called. I think he's making too much of this. I get threats all the time." The smile went away, and then came back. "Usually anonymous e-mails."

"Threatening to bomb your office?"

"That is a new touch."

"Could I see the letter?"

A ladder leaned against a bookshelf, providing access to higher shelves. The dean went up a rung or two and felt along the top of the books. He brought down the folded page. He looked at Phil. "I told the provost about this, but no one else."

"As in no one?"

"It's not the sort of message one circulates."

Phil unfolded the paper. It had been put together in the same way as the ones to the provost and the football coach, but the message was different. AcHtung! A coNtraCt

49

has bEEn taKen oUt on yOu.

"Any ideas?"

"I would say a faculty member. Because of the mention of contract. Maybe someone who didn't get renewed."

Phil asked him to explain and got more lore than he wanted about the various adjunct and auxiliary appointments to the faculty, men and women taken on for piecework, without tenure, and consequently vulnerable to being let go when the need for them lessened.

"How many people are we talking about? That didn't get renewed?"

"I made a list." He had it in a drawer of his desk, handwritten.

"You are worried, aren't you?"

"Not about violence. This is the kind of thing that can hurt the college, and the university. It would be pretty bad publicity that we have a nut running loose on campus. The fact that he or she is harmless would only add to the fun of it. From a journalistic point of view."

Oscar Wack proved more elusive. He was not in his office in Decio; there was no off-campus phone for him listed; the English department was reluctant to help.

"You've come from the provost?"

"That's right."

"And you want information about a faculty member?"

"I want to talk to him."

"Who exactly are you?"

"Why don't you call the provost's office."

But the fellow seemed to be signaling to someone behind Phil. He turned to face a spidery man of middle size with a great helmet of gray hair. His glasses were circular, the lenses thick. He looked from Phil to the secretary and back.

"Professor Wack?"

"Who is this?" He addressed the secretary.

"I'm Philip Knight. The provost asked me —"

"Knight!" He stepped back.

"Could we go somewhere to talk? It will just take a minute."

"We can talk right here."

The secretary nodded in vigorous approval.

"I don't think that would be very smart."

"What is this about?"

Oh, the hell with it. "You received a threatening letter."

"What!"

"Did you?"

"How would you have heard of that . . ."

The grayish eyes had narrowed behind the

circular glasses. He stepped back. "Knight. You're his brother, aren't you?"

"I have a brother, yes."

"So that's it.

"Look —"

"Is this part of the threat? You don't intimidate me, sir." But he backed away from Phil.

"Thanks for your time."

Wacko indeed. Phil headed for the bar of the University Club.

7

The main dining room of the Morris Inn is called Sorin's, after the founder of the university. It is a pleasant place for lunch, though crowded, but even more pleasant for dinner. Bill had introduced Mary Alice to his father in the lobby. Mr. Fenster reached out a hand, then hesitated, turned, and loped toward the dining room. He was dressed as before, but then when he traveled he carried only a duffel bag. They were shown to a table and then, as if to make up for the gaucherie in the lobby, Mr. Fenster said to Mary Alice, "I'm happy to know you."

What could she say but that she was happy to know him. Suddenly, it threatened to be a long dinner.

"I went out to the Catholic Worker House."

"Did you rent a car?"

"I took a cab."

"How was it?"

"You really ought to volunteer there, Bill."

"Catholic Worker?" Mary Alice said.

This got for her the little lecture Bill had received at lunch. What would Mary Alice make of all this?

"It would make a good article, Bill." She turned to his father. "Of course you know about *Via Media.*"

"Cardinal Newman?"

"No, no. Our alternative newspaper."

"Tell me about it."

"I can't believe that Bill hasn't told you. Wait, I have an issue in my coat." She got up and hurried from the restaurant. Mr. Fenster stirred the ice cubes in his water glass, making a chiming noise.

"Is she a good friend?"

"Yes."

"She seems nice."

"She is nice."

Mary Alice was back, got seated, and opened the issue of *Via Media* for Mr. Fenster to see. "Bill found a donor to enable us to get started. Very hush-hush."

"He wants to be anonymous." He avoided his father's eyes.

"Not many donors do. What's this about the University Club?"

"They want to tear it down."

"I didn't know there was one. Is it for students?"

"Oh, no. For faculty, alumni, townies."

Mr. Fenster skimmed the story. "Will the same donor fund the proposed new building?"

"I gather the family isn't happy about the club's being torn down. A collection of beer steins was donated along with the cost of the building. They are enshrined in cases throughout the place."

"It must have been here when I was a student. I never knew about it."

A pudgy little man had entered the restaurant and was listening to the hostess as he looked around. Suddenly his face lit up, and he hurried to their table.

"Fenster! What luck." He beamed at Mary Alice and Bill. "Have you ordered yet? I hate to eat alone."

The table could accommodate four. There seemed no way to refuse.

"My name is Quirk," the man said, as he got settled. The waitress appeared, and he ordered a scotch and water. "I hope I'm not drinking alone." Bill ordered a beer and Mary Alice a Diet Coke. Mr. Fenster said he would settle for his water. "Your father and I were classmates," Quirk said. "Well, I had a very interesting day. Do you two happen to know Professor Roger Knight?"

"We're taking his class," Mary Alice cried, delighted. "You wouldn't believe what it's about."

"F. Marion Crawford," Quirk said triumphantly. "And thereby hangs a tale."

"Who is F. Marion Crawford?" Mr. Fenster said, his voice heavy with disinterest.

"Now, Manfred, this concerns you. At least I hope it will. I know you're absolutely loaded, and this idea calls for a benefactor."

"What idea?" Mary Alice seemed unaware of the uneasiness Quirk's arrival had caused Bill's father.

Their drinks came. Quirk drank avidly, put down his glass, and hunched forward. "Listen, my children, and you shall hear."

Mary Alice would have been audience enough for the enthused alumnus, but Bill found himself caught up in this idea of using the Villa Crawford as the site of a junior year abroad.

"The place became a convent after Crawford's death, and one of his daughters joined the community. It is a magnificent structure, designed by the author himself, placed dramatically atop a cliff with the sea below."

"You've been there?"

"Several times."

"On business?" Mr. Fenster asked. He seemed to have decided to humor his old classmate.

"I'm retired, my dear fellow. On a pittance, to be sure, but enough to provide leisure to pursue my interests. I am trying to make up for the four years I wasted here. You'll know what I mean, Manfred."

Bill could not remember when he had heard his father referred to by his Christian name, one his grandmother had found in Dante, liking the sound of it, and unaware of the character it named.

"Of course Roger Knight immediately saw the brilliance of the idea."

"What will you do with the nuns?" Mr. Fenster asked.

"There are only a handful. The upkeep is funded by the Crawford estate, but it is still too expensive a proposition for a relatively small community. They should welcome the chance to move to more economical quarters. Now, Manfred, what do you think?"

"About what?"

"This would be a mere bagatelle for a man with your assets."

"You want me to pay for the purchase of this convent?"

"It is the Villa Crawford, man. It is steeped in history and tradition. Crawford lectured here in the late nineteenth century. Do you know Russell Kirk?"

"The conservative?"

"It turns out that he was a great fan of Crawford. There is even a Crawford Society. My fear is that they will have this idea and purchase the villa."

"That would make sense."

"Notre Dame must buy that villa. What do you think?"

"About what?"

"Funding the purchase."

"I never discuss money at table." Or anywhere else, in Bill's experience.

Quirk lifted both hands, as if there were something promissory in the remark. "Okay. Okay. Later. Just let the idea simmer. Talk to these two about it." He looked pleadingly at Mary Alice, and she nodded. "Good, good. What's that paper?"

Mary Alice said, "It's an alternative campus paper that Bill and I and some others put out."

"Really? I have a story for you."

He looked over both shoulders and then again hunched forward.

"There have been bomb threats. To the provost, to the dean of Arts and Letters, a faculty member, and . . ." He paused for effect. "Charlie Weis."

"No." Now Mary Alice was hunched forward.

"You remember Father Carmody, Manfred?"

Mr. Fenster looked as if he would like to deny it, but he nodded.

"He brought the news to the Knight brothers when I was there. I had heard of it where I ran into Father Carmody. He came along with me to the Knights. The brother Philip has agreed to look into it."

"Who else knows?" Mary Alice asked.

Quirk shrugged. "I don't know."

"Bill, this could be a real scoop. We have to ask Roger Knight about it."

8

Even granting he was paranoid, a possibility that Oscar Wack did not dismiss — he prided himself on keeping an open mind — even paranoids have real enemies, as someone must have said. He should remember who that someone was, but he didn't. It was a troubling realization that much of what he thought and said merely echoed what he had read and heard. But no matter, who can own an idea, or a phrase? Last week, in a lecture, he had told the story of the actress in the confessional asking the priest if it was a sin to think herself beautiful when she looked in the mirror. "No, my dear, only a mistake." Even his students had found it funny. Where had he read that? How unnerving then when the sinister Raul Izquierdo, colleague, foe, occupant of the next office, breezed into Wack's office without knocking, a Styrofoam cup of coffee held before him as if he were about to propose a toast, crying, "Congratulations."

Wack waited. There was irony and sarcasm in the very air of the faculty office building.

"You're been reading the journals of the Abbé Mugnier. *And* quoting him in class."

"I'm surprised you recognized it."

"When I myself quoted it in a recent paper?" Wack felt that he had been pounced on. As soon as Izquierdo said it, he remembered the one memorable sentence in the loathsome offprint his colleague had sailed onto his desk not long ago.

"It's hard to footnote remarks in class."

That was a counterthrust. The referees of a journal to which Izquierdo had sent one of his innumerable and unreadable articles had raised the question of plagiarism. Izquierdo had been unfazed.

"What would they say of *Ulysses,* or *Finnegans Wake*?" he had asked the departmental committee Wack had suggested look into the matter on the basis that such a charge touched on the integrity of them all. How sly to pronounce it *Finnegans Wack.*

"That they're works of genius," Wack said, his damnable voice contralto.

"Are you quoting?"

Once he had the committee laughing, Izquierdo was home free, and he knew it. It would be too much to say that Wack had made an enemy by demanding that the matter be looked into; he and Izquierdo had entered the meeting as enemies. They left the room together, Izquierdo's arm thrown over Wack's shoulders in a bogus gesture of bonhomie. "Nice try," he whispered. "I'll get you for this." The threat was made with a smile of Mexican silver.

"Why don't you take a few laps in the Rio Grande?"

"My family were landed gentry in California when yours were still swinging from trees in the Black Forest."

Now had come that absurd letter threatening to firebomb Wack's office. Its provenance seemed obvious. The disturbing visit of Philip Knight to the departmental office shook his certainty, but not for long. He bided his time, left the door of his office open, waited for the sound of Izquierdo skipping off to the men's room. He looked out. Izquierdo had left his office door open as usual. In a trice, Wack was inside. He had to try several times to get the match to light, then he dropped it into the overflowing cornucopia of Izquierdo's wastebasket. He fled the building, but as soon as he was outside his teeth began to chatter with the cold. How could he have forgotten that the temperature was only seven above? But this was no time to be fainthearted. He circled the building and entered by another door, went up to the third floor, and huddled out of sight. He could see smoke curling from Izquierdo's office. And then came the awful realization. He had left his own door open!

He pulled open the inner door and ran down the hallway toward his office. Before he got there, Izquierdo was coming toward him from the opposite direction. Who knows what might have happened if Lucy Goessen hadn't emerged from her office and begun to scream. "Fire! Fire!"

Izquierdo came to a stop at his office door and looked with horror within. Surprising himself with his presence of mind, Wack pushed past him into the office, maneuvered the flaming wastebasket into the hall with his right foot, and turned to Lucy. "Water, please. Lots of it."

All she had was a mug of coffee. Wack took it and dashed it at the flames. Meanwhile, others converged on the scene. Again Wack called for water, and this time water was brought. Soon the wastebasket was a soggy charred mess emitting an odious smell.

"This is a smoke-free building," Wack said to Izquierdo. Tentative laughter all around, and then the full-throated laughter of relief.

He distinctly heard someone refer to him as a wit. He was elated. "Better dump that somewhere."

Izquierdo glared at him with pure hatred. "You did that!"

"Put out the fire? Of course I did. Is that a sin?"

He had the onlookers with him. He felt a surge of self-confidence, the kind he sometimes felt when rehearsing his lectures before a mirror and finding them marvelous.

"No, my dear, only a mistake."

But no one heard Izquierdo. The offensive wastebasket was taken away; everyone retired to his or her respective office. Before disappearing into his, Izquierdo looked at Wack, who was seeking for some crushing final word.

"Maybe I should report this to the provost."

The unnerving memory of Philip Knight came. "What do you mean?"

"You can't fight fire with fire."

And he was gone. Izquierdo had gotten the last word. But what in the world did he mean?

9

Fred Fenster had spent most of his adult life feeling like the rich young man who had asked Jesus what he must do to be saved. "Keep the commandments." The young man already did, and so, too, did Fred. "If you would be perfect, sell all you have, give it to the poor, and come follow me." Like the rich young man, Fred had always turned sadly away from that counsel. He excused himself in part by saying that the legal complications of divesting himself of the enormous wealth his father had left him made it all but impossible. Besides, what right did he have to deprive his son of that patrimony? Bill had an independent legacy, of course, but compared with what he might inherit it seemed, in a Fenster perspective, modest. So Fred had settled for imitation poverty. He lived as simply as anyone whose sole income was Social Security. But of course it was a pretense, and he knew it, and was ashamed.

In his political phase, he had been a generous contributor to the causes he espoused, Gene McCarthy, Senator McGovern, Greenpeace; voices crying in the wilderness they had seemed, but what if they had been successful? The time came when Fred thought politics was simply a matter of misplaced emphasis. The only change that mattered was one the individual could effect in himself. He got religion, in the dismissive phrase of his sister, Vivian.

Vivian had been born to wealth and found it the most natural and agreeable condition imaginable. Her concern was the predatory forces bent on wresting her wealth and privilege from her. Her politics were somewhat to the right of what their father's had been. For her, the Republican Party had become a subservient wing of the Democrats. Her great heroine was Phyllis Schlafly, who had all but single-handedly stopped the Equal Rights Amendment. A pyrrhic victory. What the amendment sought had been gained by legislation. Pictures of women in combat gear could send Vivian into hysterics.

"Think of Joan of Arc," Fred suggested.

"Joan of Arc had a divine mission to drive the English out of France. Is Iraq a divine mission?"

He let it go. There was little to choose between winning or losing such arguments. All such things he had set aside as the things of a child. He visited Lourdes and La-Sallette; he went several times to Fatima. He brooded over the messages of these apparitions, and they endorsed his conviction that personal holiness was the answer, not collective movements. He had been surprised when Quirk mentioned Garabandal.

"Have you been there?"

"Once. It's a devilish place to find."

Fred Fenster knew. "What did you think?"

Quirk studied him. They were in the bar of the Morris Inn, Quirk drinking Bushmills, Fred with a glass of mineral water. "That place scared the hell out of me."

"That's the idea."

"Look, I made a study of several apparitions. Fatima particularly. You would think that the end of the world is at hand."

Fred said nothing, sipped his water, wondered what he was doing sitting in a bar like this. Memories of the Catholic Worker House he had visited assailed him.

"I mean, what is She saying? The world is going to hell in a handbasket. War is a punishment, and if we don't shape up, it will get worse. Well, are we shaping up?"

67

Quirk finished his drink and waved for another.

"Nothing's stopping us."

Quirk's third drink came, and he cupped it in both hands and leaned toward Fred.

"What do you think of Our Lady's university? I'm surprised you let your son go here."

"Really."

"Look, if you think this is the place we attended, forget it. Have you heard of this filthy play they've allowed to be put on here? What was the excuse? It wasn't the administration that sponsored it but certain academic departments! What a crock."

"What got you interested in Marian apparitions?"

"Remember Bastable?"

Bastable! Of course. Their classmate who had become the scourge of the Notre Dame administration. Shrewd investments had earned him the leisure to spend much of his time castigating what he regarded as the slide of Notre Dame into the status of an ex-Catholic university. Bastable had moved to South Bend, the better to be near the object of his wrath, and lived in a town house overlooking the St. Joseph River, managing his investments and firing off e-mails to one administrator or another at Notre Dame. One of the great dangers of coming to South Bend was that he might run into Bastable. Running into Quirk was almost as bad.

"Yes."

"We should get together with him."

"I can't. Not this time."

"When are you leaving?"

Fred looked at his watch. "Right now, I'm going to bed."

"Have another."

"One's my limit."

"Mineral water?"

"Did you ever taste it?"

Fred left the bar, crossed the lobby, and went up to his room, where he donned an overcoat and put on his beret. He took the elevator down, then went through the tunnel under Notre Dame Avenue and emerged in the McKenna Center. The outer doors were locked, of course, but only to prevent entry to the building. Fred let himself out and walked across the campus. The golden dome glowed in the lights trained on it; the clock in the tower of Sacred Heart looked moonlike in the darkness. He rounded the basilica and took the steps down to the Grotto, aflame with votive lights. It was a replica of the grotto at Lourdes, token of Father Sorin's devotion to the Mother of God. Fred knelt and shivered through several prayers. He had intended to say a rosary, but it was simply too cold. His prayer became an apology for his weakness.

Returning to the Morris Inn, ungloved hands thrust deep into the pockets of his overcoat, he felt himself to be a ridiculous figure. Fifty-eight years old and in many ways he still felt like an adolescent. His life seemed make-believe. Every day he read the *Liturgia Horarum,* he was a daily communicant, he longed to bring his life into line with the most austere ideal of the Christian life, but there remained the impediment of his vast inherited wealth.

Bastable. Several times, Bastable had waylaid him when he came to visit Bill. The man was a crusader. Almost literally. He was amazed that Fred wasn't a Knight of Malta.

"I'll put you up for it."

"I can't afford it."

Bastable laughed. "It turned me around, Fred. We take sick people to Lourdes, you know. That's when I first became aware of it, really."

Bastable had turned his interest in the shrine in a political direction. The messages of Mary at Fatima were a weapon he used against those who were betraying the Church. His public and private criticisms of

Notre Dame were always put forward under the aegis of what the Blessed Virgin wanted. How could anyone resist such arguments?

A year ago, Fred had accepted Bastable's invitation to stop by his town house by the river. Mrs. Bastable was a comfortable overweight woman who seemed to spend the day reading jumbo paperback novels with glistening covers. But her passion was bridge. She played four days a week, leaving Bastable to grapple with the modern world. Fred wondered what he would be like now if Margie hadn't died.

"Don't ask," Bastable growled when Fred inquired about his children.

There was a photograph of a beautiful little Chinese girl on his desk.

"My grandchild. Adopted," he added, and looked out at the river.

Bastable's reforming zeal was apparently directed only at others. He dismissed the suggestion that proximity to the campus must make daily Mass an easy matter.

"At 11:30?" he said. "Come on."

Bastable reminded Fred of himself in his political phase. When Bastable wasn't buying and selling, he was dreaming up campaigns to get the Notre Dame administration to admit their perfidy and shape up. He had known many defeats, not least with their classmates.

"They think everything is hunky-dory. Look at all the new buildings, look at what they've done to the grounds, look at Warren Golf Course."

To keep up the level of his rage, Bastable pored over the *Observer,* the student newspaper, which he called the *New York Times Lite.* "The thing might just as well be coming out of Podunk Tech. Every stupid liberal cause is championed. And the faculty . . ."

Not a happy get-together. The worst of it was that Fred came away feeling smug. *There but for the grace of God go I.* What was the point of all this rage at others if one made no demands upon oneself? Not so comforting a thought when he reflected that any demands he made on himself were voluntary and, however secret, theatrical. *I should have been a pair of ragged claws scuttling across the floors of silent seas.* He smiled, then frowned. Why hadn't a verse from the psalms occurred to him?

Roger was made uneasy when Mary Alice Frangipani and Bill Fenster came to him and wanted to talk about the threatening letters that had recently come to various administrators. "And the football coach," Mary Alice added.

"Where did you hear that?"

"Mr. Quirk suggested it would make a great story for *Via Media.*"

"I wish you wouldn't. It's not just that the provost would like to avoid the publicity. My brother would be compromised. He has been asked to look into those threats."

"How can they be kept secret?"

"Look, if you hear about them from some other source, one that doesn't involve me or Phil, go ahead. Otherwise, I really hope you won't write such a story."

They agreed — he had never doubted they would — but after they were gone, he wheeled up to his desk and made the comparison that had started dark thoughts. It seemed pretty clear that the letters pasted to the sheets of paper had been cut from an issue of *Via Media.* The font was the same, and each of the capital letters could be traced to a headline.

Roger sat and mused. After all, television networks had staged battles in order to have a scoop when they covered them. There had been too many instances of events contrived with an eye to news coverage. Of course the Fourth Estate professed shock when these were revealed, but a lesson had been taught, and Roger wondered if these young campus journalists had learned it. How better to advance the influence of their paper than to print an article about those threatening messages?

He looked again at the letters pasted to the sheet of paper. Of course anyone could have snipped those letters from the paper and concocted those messages. Those messages. It was silly to take a prank like that seriously, something he needn't tell Phil.

Phil had made the rounds of the recipients of the threatening letters.

"Are they all from the same source?" Roger asked him.

"See for yourself."

There was little doubt that the message on each sheet of paper had been formed from letters clipped from *Via Media*. The notion that the threats were an exercise in creative news would not go away.

Phil's account of his meeting with Oscar Wack seemed proof of the wild goose chase he was on.

"Is he nuts or what?"

"He teaches English."

"He seems to know you."

"I represent all that he dislikes. The amateur. I discuss books because they have given pleasure and the discussion promises greater pleasure in rereading."

"What's wrong with that?"

"Anybody can do it. Not equally well, of course, but there is no secret handshake or mystic doctrine separating the good from the best. My idea of a critic is Chesterton in his books on Dickens and Browning."

"What's the other way like?"

"You'll have to ask Professor Wack."

"I don't ever want to talk to him again."

"Don't underestimate him, Phil. He's famous in his own circles. His *Foucault, Flatulence, and Fatuity* won a prize."

"Have you read it?"

"You don't read a book like that. You decode it."

10

Two days later the special edition of *Via Media* appeared, featuring a story on the conflagration in the faculty office building. The tone was arch, the story could have been a spoof, but there were pictures of the charred wastebasket, a long quotation from Lucille Goessen, and a suggestion from Izquierdo that students read Ray Bradbury's *Fahrenheit 451*. Oscar Wack preferred to make a written statement.

The intellectual is ever under attack and nowhere more vigorously than in the university, the alleged redoubt for his ilk. A university is not a seminary or convent. Students may be unmarried but they are not celibates. The crushing suppressions of the past must be lifted. How can the mind be free when the body is not? All of us stand in solidarity with our colleague Iz-

quierdo. We will not be intimidated.
Wack, O.

That is not the way the professor had
signed his statement, and he was furious
when the issue came into his hand. He
telephoned Bill Fenster.

"Is this the office of the *Via Media*?"

"Who's calling?"

"You answer first."

"Yes."

"Professor Wack. Why are you mocking
me? For whom are you working? Who pays
for this miserable rag of a paper?" His voice
mounted as he spoke, and the last question
ended in registers audible only to dogs.

"All that is made clear in the paper."

"That you are paid to harass the faculty?"

"Professor, we didn't light the fire in
Professor Izquierdo's wastebasket."

"Someone should light a fire to you!"

He hung up.

"Maybe he'll send us a threatening message," Bill said to Mary Alice.

"It sounds as if he already has."

It was becoming ever clearer to Bill Fenster
that even a twelve- or sixteen-page paper
that appears irregularly is a stern taskmaster,
demanding much of one's time. That would

have been harder to take if Mary Alice weren't every bit as conscientious as he was. The others, well, it was a volunteer job and people came and went, but there were always enough around at crucial times. Newcomers had to be warned that they weren't interested in news.

"I thought it was a newspaper."

"No, it's a student publication. Let the others go scampering after news. We want to publish positive accounts of permanent aspects of the university. What do we know of the people who run the place, for instance?"

He was echoing his father here, of course. He could remember when his dad told him how liberating it had been when he just stopped reading papers and magazines and watching television news. The constant reader or viewer had his curiosity or indignation or anyway much of his attention engaged by some event, for the moment the most important event in the world, only to find that item replaced by another, and that by another, on and on.

"And none of them has any importance for me. More likely than not it's a distortion for sensational effect, or something I couldn't do anything about if I wanted to. How many remote weather disasters and crimes does one have to know about?"

"But how can you vote?"

"Only one or two issues are truly important, and it is easy to discover where a candidate stands on those."

His father had taken a look at *Via Media.* "It reminds me of the *Scholastic.*"

"The *Scholastic!*"

"Of long ago, when it was the sole campus publication. I like these long accounts of lectures given."

In their rivals, lectures, when they were reported at all, were reduced in the search for some controversial remark, with little sense at all being given of what had actually been said.

"You'll find no misspellings either. Thanks to Mary Alice."

Writing up the wastebasket fire in Decio had been meant as a spoof, so that was a lesson of sorts. Don't count on a sense of humor being widespread.

11

When Crenshaw of campus security showed up at the English department, he was not a welcome visitor. Hector, the secretary, eyed him warily when he asked about the fire in the building.

"It was in a wastebasket," he said.

"Your people know they can't smoke in this building, don't they?"

"No one in this department smokes!" His tone was shocked.

"I want to see the office where it happened."

"For heaven's sake. It was over before it began."

"Then why is it such a big story in this paper?" He produced the issue of *Via Media* as magicians produce rabbits.

"That rag!"

Crenshaw was getting nowhere, and he wasn't sure he regretted it. Members of the faculty sometimes treated campus security as if it represented the threat of fascism. Of course the main bone of contention was parking. With the expansion of the campus, faculty parking spots were ever more distant from their offices. No wonder that some sought to leave their cars in front of residence halls as if they were visitors. The bicycle patrol handed out tickets randomly, as traffic and parking tickets are always distributed, but Crenshaw wanted them to lean on the repeat offenders. Young Larry Douglas was a conscientious member of the bike patrol. It was too bad the fines didn't go to campus security.

A man entered, saw Crenshaw, turned, and went out.

"Who was that?"

"Professor Izquierdo."

Crenshaw went after him. "Professor, Professor, could I talk to you?"

The man turned, frowning, and looked up and down the uniformed Crenshaw. "Parking tickets are not a criminal offense."

"I'm here about the fire."

"I thought you were campus police."

"I am. Where can we talk?"

"Come in, come in." But Izquierdo entered his office first. Crenshaw looked at the wastebasket. It bore the marks of fire.

"Tell me about the fire."

"It's been written up."

"That's why I'm here."

Not quite true. Larry Douglas had come into Crenshaw's office two days before, so excited he had forgotten to remove the ridiculous helmet he wore while cycling around looking for cars parked in the wrong place so he could ticket them. Larry said he had overheard an old priest talking about bomb threats on the campus. Crenshaw had shagged the kid out of his office. The trouble with Douglas, he was so glad to have the campus job that he was overzealous. But then Crenshaw's secretary reported that there was murmuring among the staff in the Main Building about strange messages received, threatening bombs and fire. It was the story in the alternative campus paper that decided Crenshaw to look into it.

Izquierdo tipped back in his chair. "How long have you been in your job?"

"Since I retired from the police department."

"South Bend?"

"Elkhart."

"I suppose they pay you peanuts."

"Well, I have my pension, too."

"Ah, pension. It's what drives us all on. We work in order to retire. And, in your case, to work again."

Izquierdo was a funny duck. If he had seen him on campus, Crenshaw would have thought he was in maintenance. He wore faded jeans, lumberjack shoes, and a T-shirt bearing a legend that said sexual perversity was okay with him. An old corduroy jacket hung limply from a coat stand, along with a baggy winter coat and a very long and gaudy scarf. A deerstalker hat crowned the coat stand. It might have been a scarecrow.

"About the fire in my wastebasket. It was set by my colleague Wack while I was in the john."

"Why would he do that?"

"What do you know about *The Vagina Monologues*?"

"What's that?"

Izquierdo seemed surprised. "You really don't know?"

"What's it got to do with the fire in your wastebasket?"

"Intimidation."

"You said a colleague started it."

"Oscar Wack. An unbalanced fellow. He is insanely jealous of me. With reason, of course. I kept him off the committee sponsoring the *Monologues*."

"So he set fire to your wastebasket?"

"You probably find this ridiculous. It is. Life is ridiculous, when you come to think of it."

"Why didn't you call the fire department?"

"Because Wack staged the whole thing so he could look like a hero putting it out."

"Maybe I should talk with him."

"It would be wiser just to keep an eye on him."

"That isn't my job."

"I thought you wanted to know why I had a fire here."

The conversation went on like that. Crenshaw was glad to get out of there. The departmental secretary glared at him when he went by his door.

Outside, he sat behind the wheel of his car and thought of Sarasota. During his long years on the Elkhart police force he had dreamed of heading for Florida as soon as he hit retirement age. But then he heard of the opening at Notre Dame security. Crenshaw's father had served as an usher in the stadium during home football games — a visored hat, free entrance to all the games, minimal responsibilities. Notre Dame had long represented auxiliary income in the surrounding communities. The opening in security had seemed somehow a continuation of his father's connection with Notre Dame. Not for the first time, Crenshaw thought he had made a mistake in not heading for Sarasota three years ago. He knew that security was regarded as a version of the Keystone Kops. They had the equipment, a fleet of cars, the bicycle patrol, an expanding staff, the latest in technical wizardry, but they were still figures of fun. Never had he been more aware of the lack of dignity in his job than in talking with Professor Izquierdo. The man had to be stringing him along. What a great joke it would have been if Crenshaw had taken the bait and gone to quesion the colleague, Wack.

Bah. He started the engine and drove slowly away. A cop should always observe the speed limits he enforced. Except in an emergency, of course.

12

Father Tim Conway, new to the provost's office, had been assigned the task of keeping tabs on Quirk. The alumnus seemed to represent a recurring problem, as Tim gathered from talking with others in the numerous offices that housed associate, assistant, and other adjuncts to the provost. He himself was temporarily housed in an office with Roscoe Pound, a holdover from the previous regime. They had gone off on the afternoon of the day on which Tim had met Father Carmody to Legends, where they sat over beer while Pound gave Tim the benefit of his long experience.

"Quirk is a type. Check his record here as a student and you will probably find nothing. People like him drift through four years here. For most, football is their umbilical cord to campus after they graduate, but many get religion. They are the troublemakers."

"He wants us to buy a villa in Sorrento."

Pound chuckled. "I know, I know. But the idea behind it is remedial, corrective. It is a criticism of the university as it is now. He wants to bring it back to some fancied golden time. I'll bet he mentioned the *Monologues*."

"That is a pretty raunchy thing to have put on here."

"Of course it is. No decent place would allow it."

"So?"

"We're no longer a decent place. Quirk is right, but it's important not to let him know that. Look, there are three Notre Dames, the one whose history you can trace, the one such alumni as Quirk imagine, and the one we are slowly becoming."

"And what is that?"

"Read Burtchaell, read Marsden."

Tim didn't ask him to explain. "I'd rather hear what you think."

"You are."

They had another beer. The place was noisy and crowded, just the setting to receive Pound's mordant view of things.

"You were in Rome?" Pound asked.

"For four years."

"And now you've come home."

"There's a chance I'll be sent on for a

doctorate."

"Take it. One of our problems is that there are few priests of the Congregation on the faculty. The CSCs have become dorm mothers, campus ministers, supernumeraries."

"Who is Father Carmody?"

"Ah, Carmody. He is part of the history of the place. A second violinist. He goes back to Hesburgh."

"I had never heard of him."

"That is his genius. He was always in the background, whispering memento mori in the ears of administrators."

It seemed odd to Tim that he should be receiving such information about the congregation he had joined immediately after graduation from a layman like Pound. It emerged that Pound was not Catholic.

"You're surprised. I was hired by a Calvinist."

The fact that Quirk had gone off with Father Carmody gave Tim an excuse to drop in on the old priest at Holy Cross House. Here in the last stage of their religious life were the ancient members of the Congregation. Preparing for death? Most looked just bewildered and frail. They watched the young man warily as he came onto the upper floor and said he had come to see Father Carmody.

"Oh, he wants you to meet him downstairs."

The nurse offered to show him where, but Tim told her he could find it. It was while he was going downstairs again that it occurred to him that he himself might end up here someday, but the thought was as remote as old age itself.

Father Carmody looked the picture of health after the specters Tim had just seen. The old priest sat in a room where visitors could be entertained. He closed his book on his finger, then flourished it at Tim.

"Dick Sullivan's book on the university. Have you read it?"

Tim asked to see it and leafed through it, not knowing what to say.

"It is a love letter to Notre Dame. Dick signed over all royalties from it to the university. No one found that odd in those days."

"You knew him?"

"In his last years. A wonderful, gentle man. He taught English and writing. He wrote fiction himself."

"I'll have to look him up."

Father Carmody proceeded to give Tim suggestions for other reading he might do on the history of Notre Dame.

"What do they tell you people in the novitiate nowadays?"

No need to go into that. Tim turned the conversation to Quirk.

"I wish those threatening letters hadn't been mentioned in his presence," Father Carmody said.

"They're just a prank, aren't they?"

"Let's hope so. Phil Knight seems to think so. I asked him to look into it. Do you know the Knight brothers?"

"I've heard of the one who teaches."

"Roger. A whale of a man, in every sense. As learned as Zahm, and yet he wears it lightly. He only teaches undergraduates. You should get to know him."

"Tell me about Quirk."

"He's an alum, of course. Engineering. He made a modest pile and decided to retire while he could put his mind to other things. Not that he has much of a mind. Of course he is disenchanted with what the university has become."

"In what way?"

The old priest considered for a moment. "There are two schools of thought on that. One holds that we are fashioning a new way to be a Catholic university. The other holds that we are ceasing to be one."

"Which school do you belong to?"

"Both."

"How is that possible?"

"Because things are never as simple as any theory demands. The idea of buying that villa in Sorrento isn't a bad one. We're throwing money at everything else. And Quirk thinks that his classmate Fenster might come up with the purchase money. Of course there would be maintenance. Always remember maintenance when a new building is proposed. You can pay off the building, but maintenance is forever."

"The provost hasn't rejected the idea."

"If he is smart, and he is, he will wait to see if the money is there."

"Who is Fenster?"

"He's staying in the Morris Inn at the moment if you want to meet him. He's not at all like Quirk. He has mountains of money and lives like a monk. His son is the editor of *Via Media*."

Tim frowned. "Did you see the story on the fire in the English professor's office?"

Carmody nodded. "That wasn't the fellow who got the threatening letter, was it?"

"If he were, those threats could be taken as a prank. That was Wack. The fire was in the wastebasket of a professor named Izquierdo. He says Wack set the fire."

"No."

"Campus security checked it out."

"Campus security! Who told them?"

"I don't think those letters are a secret anymore."

"Ye gods."

13

His mother worked on the campus cleaning crew, each morning tidying up the rooms of male students — the women looked after themselves — part of the contingent of serfs who were all but invisible elements of the infrastructure of Notre Dame. When she had gone to work there, Mrs. Grabowski might have done better just about anywhere else, but the idea was that her employment would smooth the way for Henry's admission as a student. And he had worked his tail off at St. Joe High, just as he worked his tail off all summer earning his tuition for the year. In high school, he had gone out for freshman football and been all but laughed off the field, but no matter, his sights were ever on the SATs, which together with his mother's employment at Notre Dame would get him admitted to the student body. Mr. Masterson, his advisor, encouraged him and, when the time came, wrote a recommendation.

"Don't put all your eggs in one basket, Henry. Apply at Purdue. Apply at IU. Of course, there is always IUSB." The South Bend campus of the state university. Henry had smiled away the suggestion. It was Notre Dame or nothing. And nothing is what he got.

He had applied for early admission so he didn't have to wait for the crushing disappointment. He read the bland letter so often it was etched into his memory like the legend over Dante's Inferno. He was devastated. His advisor suggested Holy Cross College, just up the road from St. Joe High, it, too, run by the Brothers of Holy Cross.

"Lots of kids are admitted from there as sophomores, even juniors."

Henry said he would think about it. But he was filled with a terrible proletarian wrath. He threw out his video of *Rudy*. His whole imagined future was ruined. He was filled with hatred for the university that had rejected him and all his youthful dreams. His mother was philosophical about it.

"You can get a job on campus." She added, "For now."

Maintenance, maybe even campus security. She had talked to a young man on traffic patrol, a South Bend native, Larry Douglas. She actually brought him home to tell Henry of the great opportunities to be had in Notre Dame security. So Henry applied but without hope, sure it would go the way of his application to be a student. He had been accepted, to his mother's delight. When he filled out the final forms, Henry felt he was becoming a permanent member of the underclass.

He and Larry became friends, more or less. What could you think of a guy who thought riding around campus on a bicycle dispensing parking tickets made him an integral part of the Notre Dame community?

"Think of the benefits, Henry." Larry meant hospitalization and retirement. Maybe also wearing the stupid uniform.

Henry's SATs meant that he had been more than qualified for admission. He just hadn't been admitted. As he wheeled around the campus, wearing a helmet and dark glasses, he told himself that he was at least as smart as any of the carefree students he passed. Those years of study at St. Joe, the reading he had done on his own, now seemed a joke, but he couldn't rid his mind of what he had learned, and he couldn't drop the habits he acquired. He began to collect syllabi of the courses he might have taken, and read the books assigned. He got to know Izquierdo when the professor came up while Henry was writing a ticket for his misparked Corvette.

"I'm about to leave," Izquierdo said, getting behind the wheel.

"I can't just tear this up."

"Give it to me." He took the long slip and tore it into pieces, grinning at Henry. "Now you don't have to."

"You're a professor." This was clear from the sticker on his windshield.

"Is that an offense?"

"What do you teach?"

"English."

"Yeah, but what exactly?"

"A survey of British literature."

"Do you do *The Vicar of Wakefield*?"

Izquierdo looked at him. "Have you read it?"

"Twice."

"What are you doing handing out traffic tickets?"

"It's a long story."

"My office is in Decio. Come see me. But not in that uniform."

That is how it began. The first time, they talked about Goldsmith's novel, then went on to other things. Henry asked if he could have Izquierdo's syllabus. He had read half the books on the list.

"Where did you go to school?"

"St. Joe High."

"I meant college."

"I was turned down."

"Where?"

"Here."

"Geez."

On Henry's second visit, Izquierdo developed the theory that Henry was better off as he was. "Your problem is you really want to use your mind. That disqualifies you. Students are engaged in job preparation. The degree is a ticket, that's all. So-called higher education has become a fraud. Maybe it always was."

"So why are you here?"

"To dig I am not able, to beg I am ashamed. Plus, the pay is great."

For all that, Izquierdo's negative attitude toward Notre Dame rivaled Henry's own.

"I suppose you're Catholic?" he asked Henry.

"I was baptized."

"Who wasn't? This is supposed to be the premier Catholic university in the land. Give me a break."

Izquierdo had put aside the faith of his fathers.

"You're an agnostic?"

"Ha. No halfway measures for Raul. None of that can stand up to what we now know."

"What's that?"

Izquierdo looked sly. "You think I think that what I just said is true."

"Don't you?"

He shook his head. "The thing is, it isn't false either. Look, there's no there there. No objective world to underwrite our sentences and make them true or false. The world is part of what we fabricate, not independent of it. Are you following me?"

This was exciting stuff, until Henry thought of the sentence "I was turned down by Notre Dame." But talking with Izquierdo fed his conviction that he was as smart as any student. Smarter. This wobbled a bit when he found out that Larry Douglas had a secret passion for poetry, but of the obvious sort.

"Why didn't you go to college, Larry?"

"Why didn't you?"

"All it is is job preparation. I've got a job."

Larry liked that. Why didn't they double-date some weekend?

"I broke up with my girl." There had never been a girl. All that study in high school had given Henry the reputation of being a nerd.

"My girl will fix you up."

Why not?

Larry's girl was named Kimberley, a real doll, but Henry got pudgy Laura, who worked in the office of campus security. She kept telling him she hadn't wanted to come, she was only there to give Larry a bad time.

"What for?"

"Her. I was his girl for months, then she came along."

"Maybe we should trade."

Larry was driving, and he squirmed at the suggestion, but Kimberley turned and gave Henry a nice smile.

"Larry says you're quite a reader."

"Oh, a little poetry."

"Really?" Larry had given him the story about Kimberley's susceptibilities.

"Lasciate ogni speranza voi ch'entrate," he murmured.

"What's that?"

"Dante. No translation really captures the poem."

Henry knew two or three other phrases from the *Comedy,* but the one did the trick. When they got to the sports bar, Kimberley was as much with Henry as was Laura, who snuggled up to Larry.

"What other poets do you like?"

"I was just going to ask you who your

favorites were."

Larry was following this exchange with a desolate expression. Laura had him pretty well pinned in a corner of the booth, and if Kimberley was just across from him, she had turned to face Henry.

"I suppose you think Emily Dickinson is too feminine."

"No woman can be too feminine for me."

"Hey," Larry said, "how about that fire in the professor's wastebasket?"

"Let's not talk business," Henry said, but Laura was all for the suggested topic.

"And he didn't even get one of those threatening letters," she said.

"What threatening letters?" Henry wanted to know.

"That's confidential," Larry said to Laura.

"Oh pooh. It's all they talk about in the office."

"Tell me," Henry urged Laura, and Kimberley turned pouting away.

So he got the official story. The provost, the dean of Arts and Letters, Professor Wack in English, and Charlie Weis, the football coach. Henry listened as if this were all news to him. He would have to tell Izquierdo of the reaction to those messages, if he didn't already know. Izquierdo talked as if he wouldn't mind firebombing Wack's office himself.

"Look," Larry said, assuming a tone of authority. "They're just a prank."

"So why the secrecy?"

"It would still be bad publicity. Who wants such a story about Notre Dame to get around?"

Who indeed? Henry pushed closer to Kimberley. " 'I'm nobody, who are you?' "

" 'I'm nobody, too.' " And she squeezed his arm. "I love that poem."

14

The story in *Via Media* about the fire in the wastebasket of Professor Izquierdo set the Old Bastards' table aroar with excitement. Armitage Shanks felt vindicated. When he had passed on the rumor that threatening letters were circulating on the campus, he had been scorned.

"I told you so," he said with all the satisfaction the phrase conveyed.

"He probably dropped a cigarette in the wastebasket."

"You can't smoke in Decio."

"You mean you're forbidden to," Goucher corrected. "Prohibitions don't confer incapacity." Goucher had taught philosophy for forty-two years, without great success.

"He blames a colleague. Some idiot named Wack."

A wide smile replaced the vague expression on Potts's face. "Remember when we locked the dean in his private john?"

The faculty had resented the fact that the dean had a private washroom, and locking him into it had seemed condign punishment. Chuckles went round the table. Debbie, the hostess, took an empty chair, singing softly, "I Don't Want to Set the World on Fire."

"Is this a confession?"

"Are you a priest?"

"What do you hear about the conflagration in the wastebasket?"

"Just what I read in the papers."

"Maybe that's how they'll get rid of this place, burn it down."

Debbie put her hands over her ears. "I don't want to hear about it."

Armitage Shanks developed his theory that they had entered a period analogous to the phony war that had been prelude to World War II. War had been declared, but nothing much happened for months. He began to develop the parallel — the threat to the club, the countering protest, now long silence — but no one listened.

"Who was dean at the time?"

"At what time?"

"When he got locked in the john."

"Sheedy?"

"No, it was after him. Sheedy was all right. He was always hiding in the back room of

103

the museum where he could read."

"He had one assistant dean."

"Devere Plunkett."

"Have you seen the present setup? I think the dean-to-student ratio is smaller than faculty-to-student. And they're all living like Oriental satraps. I'm surprised no one has firebombed the place."

"He was one of those threatened."

"How do you know these things?"

"I make them up."

"Guess who I ran into yesterday," Plaisance said.

"In your car?"

"An old student. He recognized me, I didn't recognize him. Quirk. He asked me why no one had told him about F. Marion Crawford while he was here."

There was a long silence. Finally Shanks said, "Crawford?"

"A novelist," Bingham said, emerging from wherever he went when he tuned out. "Late nineteenth century. I haven't heard him mentioned for years."

"You haven't heard anything for years."

"What?"

Plaisance reclaimed the chair. "He wanted to know what I thought of present-day Notre Dame."

"Who?"

"Quirk."

"Is that a real name?" Armitage Shanks wanted to know.

15

Because of the weather, Greg Walsh, assistant archivist, offered to meet Roger halfway, so they were settled at a table in the pandemonium of the Huddle. A huge grainy television screen overlooked the dining area but was ignored; perhaps it was the watcher rather than the watched. Greg managed to say this, despite his impediment, but then Roger Knight was one of the few people with whom he could speak fluently.

"Big Brother." Roger laughed. "My brother Phil, that is. Can you keep a secret?"

"Could I tell one, is the question."

Roger's many references to his enormous size made it easy to refer to one's own disability.

"Several administrators, the football coach, and an English professor have received threatening notes."

Greg nodded. "I heard."

"You did?" Roger sat back. "Well, so much

for its being a secret. Where did you hear?"

"There is an alumnus named Quirk on campus who drops by the archives almost every day."

"Quirk. Of course."

"You know him."

"I've met him. He professes to have an interest in F. Marion Crawford, but all he talks about is his villa in Sorrento."

"He wanted to see any contemporary accounts of Crawford's visit here. He seemed to think all our visitors were Catholics and that the idea was to promote loyalty to our side. Sort of like football, I guess."

"He must have been reading George Shuster's little book."

"He didn't know it."

"But you told him of it."

"I'm not so sure he reads a lot, Roger."

"Early retirement is a mixed blessing."

"I'd like to try it."

"No you wouldn't."

Roger put a hand on his friend's arm. Greg had come by a circuitous route to his position in the Notre Dame archives. He had a doctorate in English and a law degree, but his speech impediment had impeded either a teaching or a legal career, so he had turned to library science and ended as perhaps the most versatile and learned archivist in the land. For the most part this light was hidden under the bushel of his stammer, but with Roger he was able to release wit and wisdom that had long been inaudible. He knew the Notre Dame archives like, in the phrase, the back of his hand.

"Did he ever explain why he is interested in F. Marion Crawford, Roger?"

"Rather than any number of other writers? No. It seems to have been a random choice. One of the novels found in a secondhand bookstore, I guess. But I really didn't press him on it. It is the villa that most excites him."

"What do the archives have on Crawford?"

Greg put a printout on the table. "Not much really interesting. But after all, a single visit."

"Everything he published is in the library."

"Well, as you know, he was the most popular author of his day."

"And the first who became wealthy by writing."

Roger himself approached F. Marion Crawford as a publishing phenomenon, perhaps the first in the country's history, although it was difficult to think of Crawford as an American novelist. He had spent very few years of his life in the United States, having been born in Rome and gone to India before he visited his uncle Sam Howe and his aunt Julia Ward Howe; two more quintessential Americans, or at least Yankees, it would be difficult to find. Most of Crawford's novels had foreign settings, Italy as often as not, but Roger had found *An American Politician* interesting if only because it recalled the time when senators had been elected by state legislators. It did not bear comparison to Trollope's *The American Senator,* but his history of Rome showed an easy erudition, as did his study of Pope Leo XIII. It was Roger's suggestion that the more typical novels — the Saracinesca trilogy — be read as deliberate alternatives to the theories of fiction of Henry James and William Dean Howells. Crawford was a professed romantic, for whom fiction commented on the human situation, not by seeking the most realistic contemporary setting, but rather by employing the exotic. It wasn't necessary to choose between the two schools, as if one were right and the other wrong. Best to take each novel by itself and analyze the enjoyment it gave. The fact that the two literary adversaries, and friends, James and Crawford had both lectured at Notre Dame fascinated, and it was disappointing that there were such scant records of the two occasions.

As with a number of his other enthusiasms, Roger's interest in Crawford had been triggered by coming upon shelves of his books in the Hesburgh Library. How wonderful to discover a hitherto unheard-of author with a shelf, sometimes several shelves, full of his books. And he could always count on Greg Walsh either to have anticipated the enthusiasm or to joyfully take it up at Roger's behest.

Roger indicated the things on the list Greg had brought that he would like to see.

"I'm not as mobile as usual with all this snow."

"I'll bring photocopies around to your place."

So they left the Huddle by the east door. Roger's golf cart was parked just outside, and a uniformed young man, his bicycle propped on its stand, was looking it over. He turned when Roger and Greg came up.

"Is this your vehicle?"

"Yes, it is."

"You can't park here."

Roger hunted for and found his permit. "I don't like to just leave it hanging on the cart."

The young man now studied the permit.

The task might have been easier if he took off his dark glasses. Roger said, "I thought you were Larry Douglas."

He took off the dark glasses. "Henry Grabowski." He handed Roger his permit. "This seems all right."

He wheeled away, and Roger and Greg sat in the cart, continuing their conversation. Ten minutes later, there was a tremendous booming sound, and Greg ran to the walk to look toward the sound.

When they came around the library, it was to see an automobile burning brightly in a No Parking zone.

PART TWO

1

"Was it insured?" Even before the odious Wack, feigning sympathy, had asked this question, Izquierdo had put two and two together. That his colleague was nuts was a given, but who would have thought he was a pyromaniac? First the stupid stunt with the wastebasket and now this. Izquierdo, his unbuttoned coat pulled tightly about him, stamping his unrubbered feet in the snow, stared at the flaming carcass of the car on which he still owed two more years of payments.

"Against being set on fire?"

"Maybe the wiring." Wack's glasses were steamed over, and he wore an idiotic smile. Maybe he was just freezing to death.

The explosion had emptied Decio and Malloy, bringing professors through the snow to the blazing car. Izquierdo had known at once that it was his, the conviction encouraged by the way Wack loped along beside him. How do you set a car on fire? How would a zombie like Wack know?

"It's a car like yours, Raul," said Lucy Goessen, joining them.

"It is mine."

"Oh my God." She moved closer. "I'll take you home."

Her place? His place? He had to be careful with Lucy. She had struck up a big friendship with Pauline, Raul's wife, and now Izquierdo got secondhand reports of what went on in Decio all day. He hadn't told Pauline about the fire in his wastebasket, it made him look foolish, but she had got a dramatic account from Lucy.

"You never tell me anything!"

"It's hard to get a word in."

Not wholly false. Pauline had a government job, downtown, dealing with drooling oldsters confused about Medicare and Medicaid. She filled his ear with pathetic tales over the dinner table, real appetizers, but as long as she was talking he didn't have to listen. He could imagine life as a long trek toward the office where Pauline worked, signing up for Medicare, on the dole at last, just when your days were numbered. Lucy's offer brought home to him what the immediate future would be like. They were down to one car, the Hummer Pauline had bought on eBay for a song.

"Hum a few bars."

"Oh ha. You're just jealous."

The reason Raul's car made such a nice fire was that it was an old, very old Corvette, all plastic. The fireman poured some kind of foam on the fire; campus security urged the onlookers to back up. Lucy wanted to know if Raul was going to tell the firemen or the security men or someone that it was his car. He shook his head. A delayed reaction came over him, a wave of melancholy memories of what that car had meant to him, the playboy professor, devil-may-care corruptor of youth. But the fun of being the unintelligible representative of continental theories had diminished because of the rivalry of Wack. At least Izquierdo knew it was a game; Wack preached nonsense with the conviction of Cotton Mather.

They began to walk back to Decio, Izquierdo bracketed by Lucy and Wack, his good and bad angels. Wack looked blue with cold and his teeth chattered. Weren't pyromaniacs supposed to get some kind of perverse thrill from observing their handiwork? Oscar looked immersed, psychologically let us say, in the icy bottom of the Inferno. The burning of the car took on Dantesque overtones, fire and ice both.

Lucy held the door for him and he went into the warmth of Decio. The gallant Wack insisted Lucy precede him. She shoved him inside and followed.

"I have coffee made."

"Good," Wack said. Lucy just looked at him.

The coffee Lucy gave them in Styrofoam cups must have been made that morning, but it was too hot to taste anyway. She went on about her coffeemaker. It didn't turn itself off automatically and sometimes she forgot to do it and in the morning, oh the smell, and the cakey gunk at the bottom of the pot.

"I normally don't drink coffee," Wack told her.

"Just abnormally?"

Wack looked at him malevolently. "On special occasions."

"Whenever a colleague's car is set on fire?"

"Do you think someone did it?" Lucy was astounded.

"I doubt that it was spontaneous combustion."

"But who would do such a thing?"

"Who would light a fire in my wastebasket?"

"But you said that was an accident."

"To protect the culprit. How could I know

what he would do next?"

Izquierdo was looking at a photograph on Lucy's bookshelf. "Who's that?"

"You wouldn't know him."

"He looks like the cabbie I rode with last week."

"It's my husband."

So the story she had told Pauline was true. Lucy turned the picture toward the wall.

Wack was thawing out, but it wasn't much of an improvement. Still, Izquierdo was glad the maniac had misinterpreted Lucy's invitation to coffee. He realized that he himself was in a state of mild shock, vulnerable to sympathy. He would be mere putty in Lucy's predatory hands. Before Pauline had got to know Lucy, Raul had been able to regale his wife with stories of Lucy's pathetic importuning. All imaginary, of course, as Pauline learned. The cabbie had proved a better audience, vicarious Leporello of Raul's amorous adventures.

"She is profoundly in love with a married man."

"What have I been telling you?"

"Her husband."

"She's married?"

"They're separated. He got mad because graduate school was taking her so long. Of course she doesn't believe in divorce. She intends to win him back."

This had been a revelation. How unobservant he had been. It turned out that Lucy attended the noon Mass in the chapel of Malloy, contiguous to Decio. Izquierdo had followed her there to be sure and lingered outside the door listening to the more or less familiar liturgy. He had half a mind to go in himself. Of course he didn't. He had lost his faith; he had destroyed Pauline's; he had no compunction about sowing doubt in the minds of his students. The funny thing was that he went on praying, addressing God as if nothing had changed between them.

"I better go." Wack had tipped forward and looked at the puddle of melted snow at his feet.

"It looks like you already have."

After Wack was gone, Raul said, "He did it, you know."

"Raul! It's melted snow."

"I mean my car. He lit that fire in my wastebasket, you know that."

"Do I? I thought it was an accident."

"He did it. Now my car."

"But that's . . ."

"I know, unbelievable. He's insanely jealous of me."

"He is."

"Over you, for one thing. You know he worships you."

"Oh stop it. Can't you be serious for five minutes?"

"Starting now?" He looked at his watch.

He accepted her offer of a ride home, just give him half an hour or so. "I won't have to call a cab."

She glared at him.

In his office he sought vainly for consolation in his unbelief. Someone was after him, there was no doubt of that, and he, too, found it difficult to think that it was Oscar Wack. He thought of all the students whose religious beliefs he had mocked. It could be anyone. He shivered. He had half a mind to start a fire in his wastebasket. The five minutes must be up. He found that he was addressing the God of his childhood.

"Don't let them get me."

2

"There's got to be a connection," Crenshaw said.

"There could be."

"That car was set on fire deliberately. There have been threats of firebombing all over the campus. Not that I wasn't the last to know."

Phil Knight didn't blame Crenshaw for being uneasy. Nor for not liking it one damned bit to be told that the administration had brought in a private investigator to look into the matter they chose to keep secret from campus security.

"Whose car was it?"

Crenshaw displayed a twisted and charred license plate. "A faculty member. He shouldn't have been parked there."

"Give him a ticket."

But he punched Crenshaw on the arm when he said it.

The head of campus security had come to

the apartment to see Phil as soon as someone in the provost's office told Crenshaw that a private detective was looking into the threatening notes that Crenshaw had learned of the hard way. Crenshaw thought there must be a connection between those notes and the torching of the car in front of the library. In the kitchen, Roger, swathed in a huge apron and sporting a Notre Dame baseball cap, was moving around in a cloud of steam making spaghetti. Meatballs simmered on the stove. This was the hour when Phil watched ESPN and argued with the experts on a sports panel, arguments he always won, of course. Crenshaw's visit, however understandable, was not welcome. And Roger had asked the head of security to stay for dinner!

Crenshaw had treated the invitation as an effort to compromise him. "I'll eat at home."

"As you wish."

Crenshaw couldn't figure Roger out. Well, few people could. Roger had already given Phil an eyewitness account of the burning before Crenshaw arrived.

"An exploding car?"

"Cars are designed to explode. Internally, that is."

Phil had been waiting for a call from Father Carmody, certain the old priest would make the connection that Crenshaw had.

Phil asked Crenshaw if he had spoken to the owner of the car.

"He wasn't in his office. I hate to bother him at home."

"How would he have gotten there?"

"Look, you're investigating this, not me. I'll leave it all to you."

That presumed that Crenshaw's presumption of a connection between the burning car and the threatening notes Phil had been asked to look into was correct. Well, maybe there was a connection.

"What's his name?"

"Izquierdo. Raul Izquierdo."

Father Carmody called after Crenshaw had gone, and Phil was able to tell him whose car had burned in front of the library.

"That's not the front," the old priest corrected. "That's the east side."

Phil told him the name of the professor whose car it was.

"I never heard of him."

"He didn't get a threatening note. As far as we know."

"Keep me posted. My dinner just arrived."

The phone went dead.

"Mangiamo!" Roger cried, and they tucked

into the spaghetti and meatballs. Phil had a glass of Chianti, and Roger, who never drank alcohol, ice water.

"Al dente," Roger murmured, approving the result of his labors.

"Do you know a Professor Izquierdo, Roger?"

"I've heard of him. One of the subversives."

"What do you mean?"

"A professor who subtly mocks in class the beliefs on which Notre Dame is built."

"You're kidding."

"I wish I was."

"Why would someone like that want to teach here?"

"Perhaps he isn't in demand elsewhere. Here he is an oddity. And our pay scale is AAAA."

"An irate student?"

Roger made the connection, thought about it, shrugged.

Roger had shown Phil the origin of the letters that had gone into those threatening messages.

"I know the kids who put out this paper. You do, too. They've been here. Bill Fenster and Mary Alice Frangipani."

"Are you saying they sent those messages?"

"No. Just that their newspaper provided the letters."

Jimmy Stewart, an old friend and detective on the South Bend police, called after supper.

"I hear you had a car set on fire."

"You busy?"

"Me? I'm a cop."

Phil had decided that he would pay a call on Izquierdo that night. Roger had approved. Strike while the car was still hot. The car had been taken downtown so that the cause of the fire could be ascertained, which is how Jimmy had heard of it. Phil had offered to pick up Jimmy, but he suggested they use public transportation, meaning his prowler. This was not the kind of errand Roger went on, curious though he was about Izquierdo. Jimmy was a grass widower and kept crazy hours; maybe that's why his wife had left him. He never talked about her, which was all right with Phil, a lifetime bachelor.

There was a Hummer in the driveway, and when Jimmy pulled in behind it, the lights in the house went out.

"Maybe we should have used your car, Phil."

They considered the situation. The fact that the Bulls were playing that night made the decision easier.

"We can talk to him on campus."

3

Larry Douglas told Laura that Crenshaw was crazy for washing his hands of the investigation into the torched car. Laura seemed to think that they were reconciled, after the way Henry had moved in on Kimberley during that ill-advised double date. Double cross was more like it. He took some consolation in the attention Laura paid to what he said. Crenshaw had shagged him from his office when he offered to investigate.

"As a parking violation?"

Crenshaw resented the fact that Philip Knight had been brought in by the administration to look into those threatening notes. Who could blame them? There were too many retired cops like Crenshaw in campus security. For them, the job was just a lark, supplementing their pension, no real police work involved. A rash of thefts in the residence hall had led to little more than a list of missing items, and a warning to look out for strangers in the dorms. Female joggers threatened on the lake paths were advised to run in pairs. This was police work? Larry, since being hired, had been reading up on criminology, police investigations, the arts and skills of the profession.

"You should have joined the real police," Laura said.

"Maybe I will yet."

Had she lost weight? That was what had made him vulnerable to Kimberley, all that flab on Laura. It hadn't mattered when they were parked and whooping it up. In the night all cows are black. Remembering her affectionate nature, to put it obliquely, he was doubly pleased with her sympathy with his criticism of Crenshaw. He almost told her that, to hell with Crenshaw, he was going to do a little freelance investigating. Finally he did tell her, since he needed her help in filching a master key for Decio.

"I'll come along."

"Better not," he said in a husky voice.

"You don't want to ride your bike, or walk. I'll get a golf cart."

"Good girl."

He bought her supper at the Huddle, and when definitive dark had settled in, they set off in the commandeered cart. They were both wearing uniforms, but who would know because of their overcoats. It was kind of snug on the seat of the cart, bun to bun, so to speak, but through so many layers of clothes it would take an inflamed imagination to find it titillating. Laura drove. The frigid wind had died down; the snow under the lamps along the walkways sparkled. Who would believe it was nearly zero?

When they got to Decio, Larry hopped out, and Laura said she would make circuits of the walkways that stretched from the library to the stadium rather than just sit immobile. As it turned out, he did not need the master key for the front door of Decio, as several professors were emerging when he got there. One held the door for him, not really looking at him. And Larry was inside.

There was a glass case to his left that listed all the occupants of the building and their office numbers. Alphabetically. He found Izquierdo, Raul. Third floor. He took the elevator up and a minute later was standing at Izquierdo's door. He had taken the precaution of telephoning the office from the Huddle. The phone rang and rang, unanswered. Still, the fact that people had been leaving the building when he came in, and the many lights in offices that had been visible when Laura drove up to the entrance, suggested caution. He knocked. Very lightly. Nothing. He was about to knock again and then thought to hell with it. He slipped the key into the lock and turned. He went in without switching on the light, shutting the door first. When he flicked on the light he turned.

"Jesus Christ!"

Henry Grabowski sat behind the desk. His look of terror when the light went on melted into mere surprise, and then he was laughing.

"You scared the crap out of me."

Larry's own heart had stopped when he turned to see the figure behind the desk. A second or two went by before he realized it wasn't the professor, for crying out loud, it was Henry. He was dressed all in black, black turtleneck, a navy peacoat, a black woolen hat pulled down to his eyebrows.

"You look like a second-story man." Larry sank into a chair, almost giddy with relief.

"Actually this is the third floor."

"What are you doing here?"

"I might ask you the same question."

"Why were you sitting in the dark?"

"I turned off the light when you knocked on the door."

"Were you here when I telephoned?"

"So that was you."

Larry's breathing was more regular now. He looked around the office. He gave a kick at the wastebasket. "It was his car that was torched. But you already know that."

Henry said nothing.

"So what did you expect to find?"

"I'm not sure."

There was a loud knocking on the door, and Larry leapt to his feet. Henry sat calmly in his chair. "Better take off the coat so they'll see your uniform."

Good idea. Of course, they were here investigating a car torching. He opened the door. An owl-eyed little man skipped backward. The uniform had its effect; the man's eyes swept over it and his indignation drained away.

"Is Raul here?" He was trying to look around Larry, but Larry blocked the door.

"Who are you, sir?"

"I am Professor Oscar Wack. I was about to complain of the noise. These walls are thin as paper." Again he tried to look inside.

"Of course you know what happened to Professor Izquierdo's car."

A sly expression came over his face. "Well, I have a theory."

"Where is your office?"

"Next door."

"Could we talk there and let my colleague get on with his work?"

"Of course, of course."

Wack scampered to his open door and inside. He looked out to make sure Larry was following.

"Better close the door," he said when Larry was inside. "Please be seated."

"You said you have a theory."

Wack nodded. "You will find this incredible."

"I'm listening." Larry settled into the chair. This was more like it, the investigating officer taking depositions.

"Izquierdo is crazy. I mean that quite seriously. He set fire to his wastebasket some days ago and blamed it on me. I am certain he set fire to his own car."

4

"It's not all that easy to burn a car," Jimmy Stewart said. "It's not just a matter of dropping a match or lit cigarette."

"*Planes, Trains, and Automobiles.*" Phil laughed, but Jimmy did not understand the allusion.

"Of course, the technique was spread all over the world in the coverage of those Arab riots in Paris."

The conversation turned to the once infamous front-page article in the *New York Review of Books* instructing on how to make a Molotov cocktail, complete with illustrations. Jimmy's point seemed to be that while it is not an easy thing to blow up a car — unless you want simply to drop a lit match into the gas tank and add self-immolation to the crime — the knowledge is easily available.

"The one safe guess is that the professor has enemies."

The two men walked to Decio from the Knights' apartment, a mistake; Phil's face seemed frozen when they reached the building. Jimmy wore a ski mask and monotonously sang "Jingle Bells" as they hurried through the arctic weather. There was an eatery on the main floor, and they stopped for coffee, if only to have something with which to warm the hands. They checked out Izquierdo's office number and got into an elevator. As the doors were closing, a hand reached in, stopping them. A little man with a helmet of gray hair reminiscent of one of the Three Stooges followed the hand, ignoring those whose ascent he had delayed. The elevator stopped on the second floor and an angular woman got out, having to push the little man aside to do so. At three the door opened and, surprisingly, the little man let them exit first.

"Can I be of help?" He was studying Phil in a confused way. He obviously only half-remembered their encounter in the departmental office.

"What's your name?"

The question altered his manner. He backed away. "Wack. Oscar Wack. Who are you?"

Jimmy showed Wack his ID, lest the professor have a stroke. He peeked at it from a safe distance.

"Others were here last night."

"Is that right?"

"A young investigator and his assistant."

"Where could we talk about this?"

"Talk about it? Haven't they reported?"

"We always double-check, Professor."

"Ah." He nodded. "Come."

He hurried down the center of the hallway but at a given point veered to one side, his shoulder brushing the wall, then into the center again.

"Here I am."

Phil sat and sipped his coffee while Jimmy got Professor Wack to talk on about his night visitors.

"I went over there because I was vexed by the noise. I mean, one works late precisely in order to have peace and quiet. You can imagine what Sturm und Drang characterize the daylight hours. Anyway, I went over there to shut Izquierdo up. God only knew what I might be interrupting."

"Oh?"

Wack made a little moist sound, then gave himself permission to go on. "Given the things that have been happening, who knows what's relevant?"

"You mean the car burning?"

"Mainly that, of course. If I were his insurance company, I would look into that matter very carefully."

"The car is being examined downtown."

"Good. I won't bore you with the story of the burning wastebasket."

"We want to hear everything, Professor, just the way you told it to our colleagues last night."

Wack's story was told with malice aforethought — he obviously hated Izquierdo — but the story had a different meaning for Phil, and he was sure for Jimmy Stewart, too. Whatever it was Wack had interrupted in Izquierdo's office, it wasn't a police investigation. Phil had stepped into the hall and called Crenshaw to ask.

"I thought we agreed, that's your problem," Crenshaw said.

"I just wanted to make sure we weren't likely to interfere with each other."

Phil went back inside Wack's office. The professor was certain the investigator he had spoken with was in uniform.

"He showed his identification." He looked significantly at Phil. His memory had kicked in. "Something you failed to do when I encountered you in the departmental office."

Suddenly Wack put a hand over his opened mouth and looked from Jimmy to Phil through his little round spectacles. He lifted his hand and slapped his forehead. "You don't think he was genuine, do you?"

"You say there were two?"

"Only the one came here to my office. At my invitation! This was to permit his partner to continue investigating Izquierdo's office."

"Was he wearing a uniform, too?"

"The second one? I never got a real good look at him."

"But you did see him?"

"I heard them before I beat on the door. There were two, no doubt about it. Besides, I saw the three of them drive away from that very window. After the interview, when he went back to Izquierdo's office, I sat on. Of course, any hope of getting anything done was destroyed. I turned off the lights. This room is quite well lit from outside, you know. Not light to read by, but it isn't dark. Very restful, actually. I was drawn to the window, the snow under the lamplight, the moon above . . ." He stopped himself. "Dear God, I sound like Immanuel Kant. Anyway, I was at the window when the cart came by to pick them up. Oh, there were two of them, all right."

"And the driver."

"She makes three, yes."

"She?"

Wack seemed to have surprised himself. "How did I know that? Yet I'm sure."

"Intuition," Phil said, and Wack looked sharply at him.

"Is Professor Izquierdo in now?" Jimmy asked.

Wack cocked his head, listening. "I don't hear anything."

"Could you telephone him?"

He pulled the phone toward him and punched out numbers without delay. Phil listened for ringing in the next office but heard nothing. Then Wack straightened and hung up the phone.

"He's there."

5

He had heard the rumble of voices next door but thought nothing of it. Lucy Goessen called to say that Wack was entertaining two middle-aged gentlemen. She had had a spy hole drilled in her door, at her own expense.

"He's insatiable. But maybe they're from the IRS."

"You know, they could be."

Or from my insurance company, Izquierdo did not say. Pauline had brought him to campus in the Hummer that morning, truly a vehicle for this season. Pauline looked like a woman on an old Soviet poster behind the wheel of the massive vehicle. Woman liberated to do manual labor. They had spent hours the night before discussing the burning of his Corvette, the topic going to bed with them and keeping Raul awake after Pauline had slipped into sated slumber.

Suspecting Wack was to flatter the idiot.

Oh, no doubt he had lit the wastebasket, but that on any scale of nuttiness was a three or four. Setting a Corvette aflame was something entirely else. Also, there was the undeniable fact that Wack had been in Decio when the explosion occurred and gone to the scene with Raul and Lucy.

The phone rang, and when he answered it went dead.

Izquierdo eased the instrument back into its cradle and stared at it. Who could blame him for being jumpy? Maybe Wack hadn't lit his wastebasket; maybe it was someone else, the someone who had torched his Corvette. There was a knock on his door.

"Come in!"

The knob rattled but that was all. He had locked his door. He never locked his door. He went around his desk and opened to two large men, the first of whom flashed his wallet and then returned it to his pocket.

"I didn't see it."

"Detective James Stewart." He let Raul study the ID.

"South Bend police."

"We are investigating your car."

These two must have been in the car that pulled into the driveway last night. Pauline had doused the lights.

"What's the point of that?" he had asked her.

She snuggled against him. At the moment, he felt as amorous as an anchorite.

Now he said, "What do you do with a burnt-out car?"

"You had insurance, of course."

"Of course." Pauline had checked that last night. But he would never find another Corvette of that vintage for any price he could afford.

"Your neighbor says someone visited this office last night."

"Wack? He's nuts, you know. Completely bonkers."

"He's quite a fan of yours, too."

"What did he say?"

"You wouldn't want us to tell him what you tell us."

Phil said, "Did you notice anything when you arrived today? Anything missing?"

Izquierdo pushed back from his desk and studied it from afar. He reached forward and opened the drawer. "Someone was in this drawer, that's for sure."

"Something missing?"

"It's the mess he made of it."

"He?"

"Whoever."

"Your colleague says there was a girl as

well as the two men."

Izquierdo made a face. Phil was certain that if Wack said that every whole is greater than its part, Izquierdo would deny it. He was looking around his office now. Then he remembered something Lucy had said and had an inspiration.

"My pogo stick!"

"Your what?"

"What I exercise with. I can do it right here. But it's gone."

That seemed to be the only thing missing. Jimmy wanted a full description of it, even a crude drawing. Phil didn't need that. There had been such a pogo stick propped in a corner of Wack's office.

"Those pretty popular here?"

"What do you mean?"

"Do your colleagues get their exercise this way?"

"Hey, this is my little secret. Can you imagine what they'd say if they saw me jumping up and down on that thing? But why would anyone take that?"

When they left Izquierdo's office, the door of Wack's office was cracked slightly. Phil gestured him out, and on the second invitation Wack emerged.

"I just want to confirm something, Professor." Phil took Izquierdo to the door of

Wack's office and pointed to the corner. "Is that the sort of thing you're missing?"

With a cry, Izquierdo sprang into the office. When he came out he was flourishing a pogo stick.

"You thief!"

"What is that? I never saw it before!"

"So you steal unconsciously?"

Wack took hold of Jimmy Stewart's sleeve. "He must have left it there last night. The investigator."

"Want to show us how that works, Professor?" Phil asked.

This flustered Izquierdo. A door across the hall opened and a lovely young woman appeared. "What on earth is going on?" She smiled when she said it.

Introductions all around. But it was the pogo stick that fascinated her.

"I haven't used one of those in years. Can I try it?"

"Watch the ceiling."

When Phil and Jimmy left, Professor Goessen was hopping up and down, with others who had emerged from their offices applauding the performance.

In the elevator, Jimmy asked, "Is everybody nuts?"

"Compared to what?"

6

At his son Bill's insistence, Fred Fenster had given Roger Knight a call and invited him to lunch at the Morris Inn. The description his son had given him did not prepare him for the apparition that needed both doors opened in order to come into the lobby. A fur cap was pulled down over his ears; he seemed to have several layers of clothing beneath the massive blue parka with NOTRE DAME emblazoned in yellow across the back. His trousers were stuffed into unbuckled galoshes, which made his passage that of a tinkling Santa. His glasses fogged up immediately, and he removed them and looked myopically around. Fred went to his guest and introduced himself.

"Fred? But isn't it Manfred?"

"I'm afraid it is. My mother had no sense of humor. Or maybe she did."

"Of course you wouldn't remember Mighty Manfred the Wonder Dog."

"Tom Terrific! Of course I do."

"So we must have similar misspent youths."

Fred helped remove several layers of clothing of his guest's and pass them over the Dutch door to the attendant. Roger's entry into the dining room commanded everyone's attention as he maneuvered carefully between the tables, attended by the hostess, several waitresses, and the amused gaze of the assembly. Roger's smile seemed meant indifferently for them all. At table Fred mentioned that his mother had mistaken Manfred for Buonconte in the *Purgatorio* when she named him.

"Saved by a single tear."

"It is my hope."

"That is the CSC motto, you know. *Spes Unica*. An anchor and cross. I think the motto has Marian overtones as well. That's clear enough in the university's motto. *Vita, Dulcedo, Spes.*"

"You'd be surprised how little I know about my university." He had known what Roger said, but it seemed humble to pretend he didn't.

"No I wouldn't. Lack of curiosity about the past of the place seems widespread. Maybe we look ahead too exclusively. What do you do, Fred?"

This was always the difficult question. He could say what he was doing at the time, as if it were a profession or a job, but he found he did not want to mislead Roger Knight. He was beginning to understand Bill's devotion to this improbable personage.

"I'm afraid I am one of the idle rich."

"Retired?"

"Well, you see, I never had to work, to earn my living. Long ago, the guilt that induces drove me into politics. I mean as a supporter. But that's long over."

"And now?"

"I am guided by my putative namesake, trying to save my soul."

Neither of them wanted a drink. When Fred ordered the Sorin Salad, Roger put down his menu. "Me, too."

"I wanted to tell you what a good influence you have been on my son."

"He is a good lad. And the newspaper he and his friends are putting out is a good thing."

Fred smiled. "The heresy of good works."

"Dom Chautard."

"You know him?"

Roger shrugged. In the lobby there were stacks of the current issue of the *Observer,* but none of the paper Bill and his friends put out. Circulation was a problem, since they relied on volunteers to distribute copies to various places around campus. At first, piles of the paper had mysteriously disappeared. In default of his son's paper, Fred had paged through the *Observer*.

"That's an amazing story about the professor whose car was firebombed."

"Izquierdo? I haven't seen it."

"I don't know when I last looked at a campus publication, but I was astounded at how matter-of-fact they were about the man's atheism. An atheist teaching at Notre Dame? He seems to be something of a missionary as well."

"Professors aren't above posturing, you know."

In reading the piece, Fred had been truly shocked. It seemed preposterous that parents would send a son or daughter to Notre Dame in order to have someone seek to undermine their faith. He could imagine what Bastable would think of this piece on Izquierdo. Of course it could be argued that one will meet with assaults on his faith throughout life and that there was little point in putting it off. An untested faith is impossible. It was quite another thing to subsidize the attack on one's beliefs.

But he had not asked Roger Knight to lunch in order to discuss campus politics.

Everything Fred had heard of the portly Huneker Professor had made him wonder if he might not, as his father had, give some financial support to Notre Dame. Quirk's campaign was having its effect. He dreaded the thought of calling on the Notre Dame Foundation, where professionals in the art of separating people from their money would have to be dealt with. What he wondered was whether he could not more or less directly underwrite the wonderful work that Roger was doing.

"Fred, I am paid far more than I am worth as it is. I sit in an endowed chair. I have a discretionary fund. There is nothing I need."

It occurred to Fred that Roger might be drawing the wrong inference from the clothes he was wearing: the same baggy sweater and corduroys with their wales all but gone. "My family has always given generously to Notre Dame. I mean my father. I'm afraid I've let that sort of thing go."

Small amounts of money, given to quite specific purposes, seemed more effective. Large sums, very large sums, seemed to satisfy some need of the giver rather than the recipient. Fred was struck by the way new buildings at Notre Dame bore the names of their donors. The pharaoh principle, more or less. Thank God his father had not been in the grip of that kind of vanity.

"In any case, I appreciate the thought. Money isn't what Notre Dame needs most just now."

"And what is?"

Roger was wedged into his chair; his napkin was tucked into his collar and lay like a pennant on his massive chest. He looked at Fred. "Let me tell you a story."

It was Roger's story, orphaned early, raised by his older brother, dubbed a prodigy, and finished with college and graduate school when most boys were finishing high school.

"Swift as my passage through college and university was, delighted as I was to be able to pursue a dozen interests at once, from the beginning I felt something was missing. You have to take a course in Dante from a professor, and a good professor, too, who shares none of Dante's religious beliefs, to know what I mean. A man can teach Shakespeare well and yet not inhabit in any way the world of the poet's real beliefs. So, too, with Chaucer, Milton, Browning. It is of course far worse in philosophy. Schopenhauer, Nietzsche, certifiably mad, read as guides to what? The tail end of modernity makes clear that it was rotting from the head down."

"So what happened?"

A radiant smile. "I read Chesterton. I read Belloc. I read Claudel. I read Maritain. Then I knew what was missing. I became a Catholic."

"And came to Notre Dame."

"Eventually. It was a bit of a shock to find almost the same assumptions and outlook that I was fleeing here. It would be too much to say that people were ashamed of the faith; the fact is, many of my colleagues haven't the least inkling of the tradition in which the university allegedly stands. They have been trained as I was and simply accepted it as the way things are. It is tragic. A whole patrimony is ignored or, when taken into account, treated in the way I found so dissatisfying."

"And you are offering an alternative."

"In a small way." He patted his middle. "Insofar as I can do anything in a small way."

Roger tried discreetly to learn just what it was Fred did with his life, how he spent his days. He dodged the questions, again characterized himself as one of the idle rich. Much as Roger impressed him, stirring as what he had said was, Fred was not prepared to speak of his religious enthusiasms.

In the lobby, dressing to face the elements, Roger wrapped an *Observer* into his clothing and then, attended once more, went outside to where his golf cart awaited him. Fred waved him off and went up to his room. A message. He checked it out and groaned. Bastable.

7

Hugh Bastable was in a rage. He paced from his study through the dining room and into the living room of the town house overlooking the St. Joseph River to which he and his wife, Florence, had moved with the idiotic notion that they would end their lives pleasantly near the institutions that, with the passage of years, seemed to have been the scene of the best years of their lives. They had come fleeing what seemed the debacle of their family. Young Hugh — he was thirty-seven now — had come out of the closet, as he put it ("The water closet!") and was now tossed about by the zeitgeist. Myrtle, their daughter, had married, three times so far, and had one neglected child for each of her discarded spouses. Florence subsided into silent resignation, but Hugh disowned them both, sold out, and moved to South Bend with Florence.

What had he expected to find? Florence

had returned from her one and only visit to St. Mary's in wordless shock. And Notre Dame! What in the name of God had happened to Hugh's alma mater? During his active years, he had paid little attention to what was happening to the Church in the wake of Vatican II. The truth was that he hadn't been much of a Catholic, too busy, too successful, too whatever. There were disquieting moments when he wondered how responsible he was for the directions his children's lives had taken. But self-knowledge was not prominent among his gifts. He needed an external enemy, and by God he had found it. Day after day, he fed his discontents, and reading the benighted *Observer* was a reliable negative stimulus. Today's issue had provided a sympathetic portrait of the professor whose car had burned near the library. Izquierdo! Was the poor fellow the victim of some bigoted student, the reporter asked? That the man was an atheist and was noted for heaping abuse on the faith in his classroom was conveyed without the least hint that there was something odd about this. Surely this was the last straw.

The difficulty was that the past three years had provided one last straw after another, and nothing seemed outrageous enough for the university to finally shape up. Bastable had scanned the story and then faxed it to a dozen kindred spirits around the country. He sent out a spam e-mail to his classmates. Florence had diligently put together an almost complete list, with e-mail addresses, that facilitated the sending of such missives. He awaited a call from Fred Fenster. But what was to be done? Bad publicity? What worse publicity could be imagined than that chuckleheaded tribute to the campus atheist? Hugh had long since canceled his pledge of support to the university. But how could you punish an institution that was the beneficiary of endless floods of generosity from the most diverse sources? To make things worse, football, after having been in the pits for years, had suddenly been turned around, and the Fighting Irish were once more at the top of the heap. Which meant more money. Was even God against him? Without three hours a weekday of Rush Limbaugh he doubted that he could go on.

No one in the administration would take his calls any longer. His letters to the *Observer* were countered by half a dozen disdainful and mocking replies, most from the faculty. One insolent young woman had suggested that Hugh Bastable was an all too fair example of the alumni the university had once turned out.

To his surprise, Fred Fenster called in person. He came in out of the cold wearing a bum's overcoat and a shapeless beret. When Florence took his wraps, there he was in a flannel shirt, a baggy sweater, and old corduroys. The man could buy and sell half his classmates, singly or collectively, and he looked as if he needed a handout.

"You got my message?"

"My, it is cold out there."

Florence offered hot chocolate, and Fred lit up like a kid. Hugh took him off to his study, what he liked to think of as his command center. On the radio a taped Rush raved on.

"Who's that?"

"You're kidding." Hugh turned it off. "Well, what are we going to do?"

"I don't know about you, but I'm going to Florida."

"We sold our place."

"Oh, I rent."

"Where?"

"Siesta Key."

"What do you do, just sit in the sun while Rome burns?"

"I walk a lot. And read."

Bastable shook his head. "Well, I can't

156

blame you for wanting to get away from here."

"I had a nice visit, actually. I had lunch today with Roger Knight."

"I should look him up. What's he like?"

"My son is taking another class from him. I can see why."

"He's not an atheist?"

Florence came in with a cup of hot chocolate for Fred. She put Hugh's Bloody Mary on the desk.

"I also went down to the Catholic Worker House."

"Is that still going on?"

"Oh yes."

"Bunch of Commies."

Fred laughed. "What will you say if Dorothy Day is canonized?"

Hugh sought consolation in his drink. St. Dorothy Day? But he could believe it. He could believe anything now.

"Sometimes I think I've lived too long already."

"You're that ready to go?"

"What do you mean?"

"I'm going to stop at Gethsemani on my way south."

The river was all but frozen over now, and swirls of snow were blowing across the surface. The trees outside the window seemed black hands groping in the wind. It took an act of faith to think they would ever leaf again.

"You ought to join. You live like a monk."

"You could come along."

"Ha!"

"What do you know about Holy Cross Village?"

This was a retirement community run by the Brothers of Holy Cross, houses, apartments, terminal medical care.

"It's right up there on top of the cliff." Bastable pointed.

"I checked it out. Maybe that will be my monastery."

Bastable was excited. "You mean settle here permanently? Great. Why, together we could —"

Fred took one hand away from his mug and held it up, shaking his head. "You know the most effective thing you could do?"

"What?"

"Say a novena."

Bastable just stared at his classmate, but for all he could tell Fred was serious. Say a novena? Did he really think . . .

Bastable stopped the thought. Of course he believed in the efficacy of prayer. The trouble was you couldn't count on it. You had to do things. But suddenly he felt helpless. Do what? Get into a rage daily and harangue Florence about what was wrong with the world? He had a fleeting image of what he had become, but he dismissed it.

"Okay. I'll say a novena. What will you do?"

"I told you. I'm going to make a retreat with the Trappists."

Bastable gave up. "You can say a few prayers to Dorothy Day."

"Good idea."

"What are you talking about?" Crenshaw demanded, when Jimmy Stewart asked if campus security had found anything interesting when they checked out Izquierdo's office.

"The inspection of the car turned up nothing. The professor himself was of no help. But you found nothing?"

"That is all in Phil Knight's hands."

Jimmy thought about it, then let it go. If Crenshaw wasn't interested, then he and Phil could find out who Oscar Wack had found examining Izquierdo's office. That it wasn't imaginary seemed proved by the presence of the pogo stick in the wrong office. Why had he thought of that young guy in the space-cadet helmet when Wack had described the supposed investigation going on in Izquierdo's office?

More snow was falling. What a winter this was. Phil had asked him out to watch a game, but the weather made that less attractive. Of course he would go. The thought of watching the game alone suddenly brought home to him what a lonely life he led. Not that he was given to self-pity. It hadn't been a shot in the arm to his self-esteem when Hazel told him she was going. He found himself unable to think of any good reason for her to stay. Her complaint was that he was too wrapped up in his work, but of course it was because they had no kids that her life was boring. He had suggested adoption, but she just made a face and wouldn't talk about it.

When he put down the phone after talking to Crenshaw, he wondered if that was his destiny. Get his pension and then apply for a job at Notre Dame security. Any real problems were foisted off on South Bend anyway, or lately on Phil Knight. He looked around his office and thought of Oscar Wack. Is that the way he looked to other people, a quirky bachelor? Geez. He got up, put on a storm coat, and headed for the elevator. He would waste the time before going to Phil's in a bar on Grape Road.

Downstairs he ran into Piazza, stamping snow from his shoes and looking around as if trying to keep time to the Muzak. He was in uniform; he preferred being in uniform, saying it saved on clothes. Piazza was always being kidded about using the prowler he took home as the family car. But he couldn't have got half his family in the thing, there being seven little Piazzas. They kept him on patrol duty because it was safer and because that was what his wife wanted. Sitting at a desk would have kept him out of harm's way, but Piazza would have none of it.

"Look, I was a clerk in the army. I had my fill of that."

He looked as if he had had his fill of lots of things, a real roly-poly. But then his wife was a terrific cook.

"Come watch the game tonight, Phil."

"I wish I could, Lou." And he did. It was hectic at the Piazzas', with all those kids, but the place was what a home should be.

"Big date?"

"I'll never tell."

"Ho ho."

Outside and through the snow to his car. Had Lou been kidding? Did others think he led an interesting life, now that Hazel had gone to California? There were times when he really missed her, even the nagging. He should give her a call. Of course she was still single. They had been married at St. Hedwig's, a big Polish wedding with a huge supper and dancing until all hours. How could you ever feel unmarried after a shin-dig like that? And of course they were Catholics. At first he had thought that Hazel would miss him the way he missed her and they would get together again. That was still possible, but the more years you added to a separation the more likely it was it would go on. Separation. That was all her pastor, old Senski, would permit her, and he had been against that. It had been something to watch the expression on the priest's face while Hazel tried to explain how awful her life was.

"You think I never get bored? What if I decided to just toss in my cards and go?"

"Well, at least you get to Florida in the winter."

"Take her to Florida," Senski had advised Jimmy.

"I don't want to go to Florida. I want a life of my own."

"Why no kids?"

"It's not my fault." She broke down then, crying like a kid. It broke Jimmy's heart to see a grown woman do that. From that point on, Senski's sympathy was with Jimmy, but that meant he was going to let Hazel call it a separation and head for her sister's in Santa Monica.

It took him fifteen minutes to scrape the

ice off the windows. That was probably the most exercise he'd had all week. Maybe he would get a pogo stick and bounce around the house.

He had a couple of lonely beers before heading for the Knights', where Roger had made enough goulash for John Madden. Phil had laid in a supply of Guinness for the game, and during the hyped-up intro, with the set muted, Jimmy asked Phil if he remembered that kid on campus security that had been a help when they were on the Kittock murder. But it was Roger who remembered.

"Larry. Larry Douglas."

9

Quirk had asked to audit Roger's class on F. Marion Crawford, and Roger had countered with the suggestion that Quirk give a guest lecture.

"I never taught a day in my life."

"It's just a matter of discussing with other people some topic you know better than they do."

"I'm not making any headway with the provost."

Father Carmody felt that he was getting a secondhand run-around himself insofar as Quirk had been turned over to him. Now, as a result of the dilly-dallying, they had lost the chance to put the proposal to Fred Fenster. Of course Mendax in development had checked out Fenster and came back whistling and rolling his eyes. Neither Quirk nor Father Carmody had needed such confirmation. Father Carmody had of course remembered Fenster. He had been very active in campus politics on the liberal side and kept it up after graduation. He could afford it. Carmody knew Manfred's father, a gentleman of the old school, as only his friends would have put it. All the confidence of the self-made man. But he had been generous to Notre Dame so long as you listened first to his extended exposition of what was wrong with civilization. Unlike others, he had never included Notre Dame in his negative estimate of the modern world. Father Carmody could still remember old Fenster's eye damp with sentiment when he returned for home football games and was included in the select group entertained in the presidential aerie on the fourteenth floor of the library.

"Roger," Father Carmody said, bringing the Knights up to speed, "the problem is that Quirk wants to be generous with someone else's money. I suggested that he pledge something himself, to get the ball rolling. He thinks he's being stalled."

"Maybe he can't afford it."

"Ha. He's no Fenster, but he's got plenty."

"I'm surprised he hasn't just gone ahead and bought the villa in Sorrento."

"He tried to."

"He did?"

Carmody nodded. "Given the use to

which it had been put in recent years, they want to turn it over to a religious order. So he asked, how about the greatest Catholic university in the world? They liked that."

"But he could have bought it himself?"

"I know what you're thinking, Roger. Why not just fork over the purchase money to Notre Dame and leave Fenster out of it? Sometimes I thinks he wants the project to fail."

"Has he been generous to the university?"

"Not lately."

Notre Dame alumni all looked alike at first, and then they fell into types and subspecies and ultimately into fierce singularity, no two really alike. Roger had classified Quirk among the nostalgics, and there was something to be said for that. His voice could get husky when he spoke of his time on campus. But he had a lot in common with what Roger thought of as alumni-penitents, men and women who bewailed the fact that they had wasted their undergraduate years. Some of these, like Quirk apparently, resolved to do belatedly what they had not done in their youth. But F. Marion Crawford, fascinating as Roger himself found the author, was an odd handle to take hold of initially. Then Roger began to suspect that Quirk's knowledge of the author was fairly superficial. He hadn't actually read much by Crawford. He had found *Ave Roma Immortalis* tough going, and of the novels he had read he preferred *The Ralstons!*

"Fred only reads saints and mystics," Quirk had answered when Roger asked him what headway he was making with Fenster. That had made Roger curious and he had gladly accepted Fred Fenster's invitation to lunch. And now the mysterious alumnus was gone.

"That's the way it always is," Bill said. "He shows up without warning, and then one day he calls to say so long."

"How often does he come?"

"A couple of times a year. His life is pretty much his own, you know."

Mary Alice said, "I think he really liked *Via Media.* Except for the symposium on abortuaries."

The question was, can force be used to protect innocent life, and one or two participants had been all for marching on the clinics and forcibly shutting them down. Even burning them down. The consensus had been against that, thank God. But to the zealous young it seemed a counsel of accommodation to recommend the slow path of legislative reform. The trouble was that the flood of abortions had not been begun by the passage of any law. Roger could share the anguish, who could not?

"What did your father say?"

"He said that in his experience any attempt to change others usually led to something worse."

"He suggested prayer and penance," Mary Alice said. "No one could stop us from doing that."

Quirk, on the other hand, applauded the more fiery contributions to the symposium. Not that he wanted to defend the position.

"It's just a gut feeling," he told Roger.

"Civil disobedience. Like Dorothy Day?"

That was sly, of course. Roger had gotten some sense of where Quirk stood on the Catholic Worker movement when Quirk mentioned that Fred Fenster had paid the local group a visit.

When eventually Quirk did show up for Roger's class on Crawford, he sat in a corner and said nothing, following the discussion but not taking part. He stayed around afterward, and it seemed that he had come to the class largely to talk with Roger.

"Did you know there's an atheist on the faculty?"

"You've been reading the paper."

"I can't believe it. It's not just what he

might or might not believe himself. He preaches it in class."

Roger disliked feeling this kind of indignation. Quirk was puffed up with rectitude, a defender of the faith. Well, no need to doubt his sincerity. But Roger could understand why Fred Fenster had withdrawn into quietism.

10

Oscar Wack gnashed his teeth in indignation. The story in the campus paper featuring Izquierdo should have been the kiss of death. Instead he was being hailed as a hero of academic freedom. The intrepid atheist. And he had stolen Wack's thunder! That hurt. That and the realization that he himself would not have had the guts to bare his soul to a student reporter. Now, of course, the burning of Izquierdo's car was seen as an attack on a man who had the courage of his convictions.

How accommodating could the university be? Did they imagine that a Holocaust denier would be feted at Brandeis? You could understand all the waffling about *The Vagina Monologues* and other activities of campus gay groups. To oppose those would invite being pilloried by the national media. That would have been a real clash of creeds. And Notre Dame blinked. But for God's sake, how could you sit still for a professor who used his classroom to argue atheism and mock Catholicism? If that wasn't rock bottom, Wack didn't understand the faith of his fathers. Yet Izquierdo was a hero.

Huddled at the desk in his office, muttering to himself, Wack asked half aloud when that blimp of a Roger Knight and his obsequious minions would take on Izquierdo. After Izquierdo, Roger Knight was Wack's greatest complaint. So he had earned a Princeton doctorate when he was still using a teething ring; he had never held a teaching position, and his reputation reposed on a single monograph, the incredibly successful little book on Baron Corvo. That was the unkindest cut of all. Wack had long nursed a secret passion for the writings of Corvo. Not the sort of thing you could admit in the department, of course. Wack had every biography ever written on the tragic author, beginning with Symonds's *Quest for Corvo.* The man had fascinated many, but they were all outside the walls of academe. No matter. When his disbelief wobbled, Wack could curl up with *Hadrian VII* and feed his disdain for the church that regarded what was delicately called his sexual orientation as sinful. It had been the thought of subjecting himself to the humiliation of the confessional that had opened Wack's mind to the flaws in any proof for the existence of God and liberated him from the faith.

Of course his personal life was concealed behind the armor of indirection. Never anything overt! Stolen holidays, trying to live out his convictions in the Caribbean sunlight but always hampered by the repressive beliefs of his youth, that was as much as he dared. On campus Wack was as chaste as a Trappist and kept all crusaders at arm's length. Izquierdo, of course, was flamboyantly heterosexual, and Wack was not misled by the man's lip service to sexual liberation in the fullest sense. Izquierdo had guessed his secret, he was sure of it, though the taunting was always ambiguous enough. Item, his teasing of Wack about Lucy Goessen.

"Of course I know the impediment," Izquierdo had said, his eyebrows dancing. Wack was furious. Was this a reference to his lisp?

"She's married."

"I didn't know that."

"Isn't that what holds you back?"

Oh, the homophobic beast. But it had drawn him closer to Lucy. How buoyant she had been when she displayed her agility on the pogo stick that had somehow ended up in Wack's office. That memory led on to the memory of that late-night investigation of Izquierdo's office. He sat back, and some of his anguish left him.

Were they on to Izquierdo, after all? Were they looking for something that would provide an oblique way of bringing the man down? Of course. Why take him on frontally and turn him into a martyr of academic freedom? Everyone is vulnerable in a dozen ways. Wack shivered at the thought of anyone rummaging through his office. It was sneaky, of course, entering an office when the building was empty for the night, or so they thought. What if someone else had come upon them, someone other than Oscar Wack? The enemy of my enemy is my friend. What did Lucy make of all this?

He went downstairs for a sandwich and saw Lucy huddled with a man at a table in the lobby. Oscar studied them as he moved slowly through the line. The man wasn't faculty, and he was too old to be a student. The conversation seemed anything but casual. Oscar made a beeline for the table when he had his sandwich and milk.

"Lucy!"

She looked up at him, startled. Oscar pulled out a chair, smiling at her companion, and got a cold look in return. "I'm Oscar Wack. Lucy's colleague."

"This is Alan," Lucy said.

The man nodded and pushed away from the table. "I've got to get back to work." And he was gone.

Oscar was dying with curiosity but decided on indirection. "Have you seen Giordano Bruno today?" he asked Lucy.

"I know I should understand that."

"His statue is in the Campo dei Fiori. Burned at the stake for heresy."

"You mean Raul?"

Good Lord. But she did have a mind of sorts. Several solid articles on Kate Chopin.

"I didn't know he had a daughter," Izquierdo had said.

"Oh you."

"You think he's kidding?" Wack had intervened.

But there was no point in trying to score on Izquierdo, not when there were witnesses.

"I wish the weather would break," Oscar said.

"I've gotten used to it."

"If it gets too cold you can always touch a match to your car."

She leaned toward him. Honey-colored hair, green eyes. Had he ever seen green eyes before? "Do you think there is a connection?"

It had been a mistake to make Izquierdo the topic of conversation, but he had no gift for small talk. "Who's Alan?"

She seemed to be considering several answers. "A friend."

"Is it true that you're married?"

She sat back and stared at him with wide eyes. "Who told you?"

"Told me? It's not a sin."

Tears were leaking from her green eyes. And suddenly she was telling him all about herself; his gaucherie had proved the open sesame. Her husband initially backed her graduate studies, then came to resent them, finally saw that he would look like an appendage, and left.

"What does he do?"

"Do?"

"I mean workwise."

She lowered her voice. "He has a chauffeur's license." Her chin lifted. "He drives a cab."

"Tell me about it."

It was another world, but talking about it removed a barrier between them. He could imagine their becoming friends, even good friends. Brother and sister. Maybe he could be instrumental in bringing her and Alan together. The idea had the attraction of seeming aimed against Izquierdo. But all that would have to wait. She was off to class then, and Wack went up to his office.

His phone rang, and Hector, the departmental secretary, asked if he had seen Izquierdo.

"Did you try telephoning his office?" he said huffily.

"No answer. His wife is looking for him."

Hector hung up before Wack could slam the phone down. What insolence. After a minute, he stood and put his ear to the wall between his office and Izquierdo's. He could hear nothing, but then he wasn't answering his phone. If he was in there.

Wack opened his door and looked out at an empty corridor. He slipped next door and wrapped his hand around the knob of Izquierdo's door. He turned it and the door began to open. That was a surprise. One didn't go away and leave the door of one's office unlocked. Not that investigators couldn't invade if they wanted to. He pushed the door open, flicking the light on as he did.

Izquierdo sat behind his desk, staring at Wack. Or staring at anything that looked at him. He didn't move. He said nothing. Wack had moved one foot back, preparing to flee.

"Your wife's looking for you."

The expression did not change. A horrible thought occurred. Wack moved closer to the desk. The eyes never blinked. He reached out tentatively, prepared to scoot if Izquierdo was putting on an act. Then his fingers came in contact with Izquierdo's forehead. It was ice cold.

With a shriek, Wack bounded into the corridor and began to spread the alarm.

■ ■ ■ ■

PART THREE

■ ■ ■ ■

1

When the South Bend paramedics arrived on the scene, the Notre Dame fire department was already there, and campus security was trying to cordon off the area on the third floor of Decio where the dead body of Raul Izquierdo had been found, seated behind his desk, staring blankly into eternity. Professors objected to this invasion of their space, of course, and diplomatic skills were called into play. Those having failed, everyone was chased from the floor and a burly sergeant was put on sentry duty.

Flashes of light from the open door of Izquierdo's office indicated that photographs were being taken. When Phil Knight arrived, the sergeant waved him through to a murmur of disapproval from onlookers. Phil found Jimmy Stewart in the office, watching the technical recording of the crime scene.

"How'd he go?" Phil asked.

"He looks as if he was scared to death."

"Why don't they shut his eyes?"

"Later."

Photographs having been taken, the desk and most of the office dusted for prints, the coroner pronounced Izquierdo officially dead. When he headed for the door, Jimmy stopped him.

"Well?"

"I'd say strangled."

"With what?"

"There's nothing here."

When Crenshaw arrived he had trouble getting past the sergeant and was in a mood when he confronted Jimmy. "No one called me," he complained. "The sight of all that equipment was my first realization anything had happened." They turned as a gurney with the zipped-up body bag rolled past. Crenshaw stepped back.

"Is that a body?"

"Professor Izquierdo."

"Good God." He thought. "I cede jurisdiction to you."

Jimmy let it go. There were lots of invisible curtains between town and gown, but dead bodies were not a university affair. Crenshaw looked around, then headed for a water fountain. It was almost a relief when he dipped to drink. He might have intended to symbolically wash his hands of the whole business. He came back.

"Izquierdo is the guy whose car was burned."

Jimmy nodded.

"You going to represent the university?" Crenshaw asked Phil.

"I guess."

"You guess?"

"I haven't talked to Father Carmody yet."

Crenshaw unclipped a cell phone and handed it to Phil. Well, why not? Phil punched out the number of Holy Cross House and asked for Father Carmody.

"He's taking his nap."

"Lucky him. This is important."

A pause. He was asked to wait. While he did, Phil took Crenshaw's cell phone down the hall a bit. The sergeant was still keeping the faculty at bay. There had been a lull when they realized what was on the gurney that rolled by them, but now the grumbling resumed. Jimmy went to tell the sergeant it was okay now. Father Carmody came on, his voice cranky.

"Phil Knight. We have a body in Decio."

"Decio is full of bodies."

"This one is dead."

Silence. "Who?"

"Raul Izquierdo."

"The atheist?" A beat. "Well, he isn't any

183

longer. Tell me about it."

"Things are still fluid. Crenshaw asked if I represented the university in this."

"Of course you do. It's a continuation of those damned notes, isn't it?"

No point in telling Carmody that Izquierdo hadn't received a note. At least he had never said so.

"I'll come by later with what we learn."

When Phil got back to Jimmy and Crenshaw, Jimmy had just asked the head of security if Larry Douglas was around.

"Douglas? What for?"

"Where can I reach him?"

Crenshaw took the cell phone, called his office, and said, "Laura, where is Larry Douglas?" He listened, frowning. He folded up the phone.

"He called in sick."

"Is he a local boy?"

"You got a dead man here and you wonder about some kid who dishes out parking tickets?" But Crenshaw seemed to remember how Douglas had outshone him in the Kittock killing. "I'll let him know you want to see him."

"No need to do that. I was just curious."

"Sure you were."

Crenshaw wheeled and went down the corridor at a great rate. There are cops and

184

cops, and Crenshaw was the other kind. Jimmy put the sergeant on sentry at Izquierdo's door and was about to go in when he hesitated, then went and knocked on the door of the adjacent office. He had to knock three times before there was the sound of a lock turning, the door opened slightly, and a terrified face looked out. "Professor Wack?"

"Yes, yes. What is it?"

"You found him, right?"

"Is he . . ."

"Yes. The body's been taken away."

The look of terror increased, then subsided as Wack slumped to the floor.

They pushed in, picked him up, and got him into his desk chair. He was white as a sheet and still out. Jimmy picked up a container half full of cool coffee and dashed it into Wack's face. He came spluttering to consciousness. He looked wildly at Jimmy and then began to dab at his shirt with a handkerchief.

"Tell us about it," Jimmy said.

The narrative gift is unequally distributed, and even those who normally have it can lose it in a pressure situation. Wack babbled more or less incoherently. Jimmy sat, and Phil did, too.

"Look," Jimmy said. "Did you ever make

a general confession?"

"What?"

"The confessor runs down the list and you say yes and no. I'm going to do that, okay?"

Wack nodded.

"You discovered the body?"

"Yes."

"You went next door, walked in, and there he was behind the desk?"

Wack nodded, then closed his eyes. He opened them right away.

"Why did you go over there?"

He couldn't answer yes or no to that, but now he was less agitated. "The departmental secretary said his wife was looking for him."

"What's her name?"

"Him. Hector. A pardonable mistake."

Phil said, "Has she been told?"

"Professor," Jimmy said, "why don't you call Hector and have him call Mrs. Izquierdo. Just tell her something has happened."

Wack picked up his phone. Izquierdo's death apparently came as a surprise to Hector, so Wack told him what had happened.

"Yes, dead. At his desk. This place has been simply crawling with firemen, policemen, detectives, what-all. Just call her, all right?" Pause. "I understand. Just tell her that something has happened, that's all you have to say. And she should come at once."

Wack's eyes widened, and he looked at Jimmy. "Where should she come?"

"Campus security." Jimmy avoided Phil's eyes.

Wack repeated it, then hung up.

"So, Izquierdo's wife calls Hector and says she can't reach her husband?"

"Words to that effect."

"We'll speak to her later. So what did you do then? Go right next door?"

"Not immediately. No. But soon."

"You knocked?"

"The door wasn't locked."

"You tried it?"

"Yes."

"Having knocked?"

"I don't remember."

"And there he was, seated at his desk?"

"Staring." He shuddered. "I noticed his eyes didn't blink. I touched his forehead . . ."

And then he spread the alarm. Wack had no idea when Izquierdo had arrived in his office; he had been unaware of his even being there throughout the morning.

"Keep these memories fresh," Jimmy advised him. "We'll talk again."

Phil and Jimmy then went to Izquierdo's

office, where Jimmy took the desk chair and began slowly to rotate it. Phil was looking at the spines of the books all neatly stored in their shelves. He said, "He should have put up a struggle if he was strangled."

Jimmy bent over and looked at the well of the desk, then studied the floor. "I think maybe he did. Unless he just enjoyed kicking the hell out of his desk. And you can see that the desk is not sitting in the indentations it made in the carpet. Whoever killed him must have tidied up before he left."

The plastic bag containing snippings from *Via Media,* a pair of scissors, and glue was in a bottom drawer of the desk. Jimmy removed it carefully and laid it on the desk, its contents visible through the clear plastic. He looked at Phil.

"No wonder he didn't get a threatening letter himself."

"Return to sender?"

They left the office in the care of the sergeant and took the elevator downstairs. Jimmy's car was parked on the sidewalk in front of Decio; when he came, he had just hung a left from the stadium.

When they were buckled in, Phil asked, "Why did you ask Crenshaw about that kid Larry Douglas?"

"Let's go see."

2

The loft Larry had rented after being hired by Notre Dame security was not much — his mother had wept when he showed it to her — but it was exactly what he wanted, a big room and no one to tell him to clean it up. The bed was emperor size at least, and he lay on his back in the middle of it staring at the ceiling. There was an overhead fixture with a fan that sounded like an airplane in trouble when he turned it on, something he didn't do in this kind of weather. He had two windows right under the eaves from which icicles hung now, glittering in the weak sunlight. The television was a reject of his parents', but he only used it for sports, and then he preferred a sports bar with Laura.

Laura. The interlude with Kimberley had been too good to last; she had deserted him for Henry, who had a line like Don Juan. Some contest. Don Juan and Don Quixote.

So he was stuck with Laura again. She loved this loft, not that he let her up here very often. Any grappling had to go on elsewhere, usually in his car. He might be on his own, but his mother's presence hung over the loft like a persistent conscience.

The sad thing was that, once he had exchanged Laura for Kimberley, he had repented of those prolonged sessions in the car, and one day he went to Sacred Heart at eleven in the morning, his uniform concealed by a bulky jacket, and got in line at the confessional. He was still trying to figure out how to tell the priest when his turn came. As soon as the grille slid open, he blurted out that he had committed adultery.

On the other side of the grille, the priest stirred. "You're married?"

"No, Father."

"The woman is married."

"No."

A pause. "You had relations with her?"

Larry relaxed. The priest had been startled by the way he began, but this was his job. He said yes, he'd had relations with her.

Just the once?

"Many times."

"Three, four."

"Dozens of times."

Another pause. "Is she a student, too?"

"I'm not a student, Father."

"I see." He sounded relieved.

Kneeling during the long pep talk that followed, Larry began to think of the others waiting in line. How long had he been in here? He assured the priest that he had stopped seeing the girl, he meant never to see her again.

"Good. Good."

For his penance he was to say Psalm 32; he would find it in the red book in the pews. Would he do that?

"Yes, Father."

And then he was given absolution. He practically floated out of the confessional, drifting past those in line, avoiding their eyes. He went halfway down a side aisle and slid into a pew. How easy it had been. He sat, staring at the altar, at the statue of Mary in the niche high above on the back wall. He had recited the Act of Contrition before receiving absolution and promising to amend his life; that meant that from now on it was Kimberley, because Kimberley wouldn't allow him the liberties Laura had. He took out the red book and found the psalm.

That had been a month ago, and now, thanks to Henry, he was back in the danger area. Laura had reclaimed him with familiar warmth; he had let her tell him what a shallow person Kimberley was, just the sort of person someone like Henry would find attractive.

"You had a narrow escape, Larry."

Escape was what he thought of as they huddled in the front seat of his car. Laura did a lot of sighing that sounded phony to Larry. He was the phony, though. It wasn't just with Kimberley that Henry had asserted his superiority. He had come to treat Larry like an apprentice, even though they had been hired within weeks of one another.

On Sunday he had gone to Mass with his mother, and she didn't exactly quiz him about not receiving communion, but he could hear the wheels turning in her head. After dinner, she wondered if she shouldn't give that loft of his a good cleaning. It brought back memories of how she had prowled around his room when he lived at home. He didn't have to wonder what she would think of Laura. All that meat and no potatoes. He had come back here to his loft, alone, and told himself he had to go to confession again. He would know enough to call it fornication this time. But what was the point? He couldn't shake Laura, so he couldn't promise to amend his life. He felt miserable. That morning he called in sick.

"Oh, that's a shame," Laura said.

"I'll be all right." But he said it with a croaking voice.

"I'll stop over after work."

"No, no. That's okay." He added, "I don't want you to catch it."

"What is it?"

"Flu." Short for influenza. Influence. Bad influence. Lady, beware.

The thing about faking illness, you began to feel sick. So he had lain in bed, the covers pulled up to his chin, and stared at the blades of that stupid fan above.

When Laura called again he had actually fallen asleep.

"They found Professor Izquierdo's body in his office." Laura said it in a whisper as if she didn't want to be overheard.

Larry sat up like Lazarus. "What do you mean?"

"He's dead." She was still whispering.

He listened to her garbled account, sitting on the edge of the bed. Of all the days not to be at work! The South Bend police had been called, of course, and Larry would bet that meant Stewart. Stewart had liked him, had treated him with respect, and Crenshaw hadn't liked it, but to hell with him.

"I'm coming out," he said.

"With the flu? You stay right there."

How could he tell her he was faking? Then she was whispering again.

"I just hope they don't find out you know what."

"What?"

Of course he knew what. Laura had filched the master key for Decio and gone over there with him. Henry! My God, whenever he thought of opening that door and seeing Henry, dressed all in black, sitting at the desk, the hair on his head would almost lift.

"Yeah. Look, Laura, keep me posted, will you?"

"Of course. But get some rest."

Are all women mothers? Well, Laura was one big mama, that's for sure.

He showered and shaved, his ear cocked for the phone; he dressed and had a bowl of cereal as if it were morning rather than early afternoon. When the phone rang he flew to it.

"Yes."

"Larry Douglas?"

"Who's this?"

"Detective Stewart. I understand you're feeling under the weather."

"It's nothing. I feel much better." Did Stewart want his help?

"Could we talk?"

"Absolutely. Where?"

"What's wrong with there?"

"Not a thing. Come on over."

He hung up, looked around the loft, and began to straighten things up. He threw armfuls of clothing into the closet and closed it. He made the bed, more or less. He looked at all the dishes in the sink but decided against doing them now. He spent the time before Stewart arrived pacing the loft. Maybe it was just as well he had called in sick. Crenshaw would have done anything to prevent Stewart from consulting with Larry. He realized he was smiling. He hadn't felt this good since he had come out of that confessional cleansed of his sins.

"Quite a place," Stewart said, when Larry let him in. Philip Knight was with him, and Larry was certain they were going to ask his help.

"You've heard about Izquierdo?"

He nodded, looking serious. "They called to tell me."

"How you feeling?"

"Much better. It must have been one of those quick bouts."

"You're sure?"

They went down to the car, and Stewart put Larry up front with him, while Phil

Knight sat in back. The streets were a mess, icy snow, and the day was gloomy again, but Larry felt great. What were the chances of becoming a real cop? Maybe Notre Dame security would be a farm team from which he would rise to the majors. From the backseat, Phil Knight talked about the crime scene. That was where they were headed. Larry was glad he had put on his uniform.

Larry was a little startled when Jimmy just swung onto the sidewalk and glided along to the front of Decio.

"I won't give you a ticket," he said when Stewart had parked.

A big laugh all around. Larry felt terrific, a member of the team. They had come for him to ask his help! Wait until Henry heard of this.

Up the elevator and down the hall, three detectives on duty. The sergeant stepped aside, but Stewart went past Izquierdo's office and knocked at the next door. He had to knock again before Professor Wack opened. He looked annoyed, he looked frightened, and then he looked at Larry. His eyes narrowed.

"You put that pogo stick in my office!"

Stewart said, "You recognize this officer?"

"Of course I recognize him."

Larry felt as if someone had kicked him in

the stomach. The memory of that crazy night when he had let himself into Izquierdo's office, when Wack had interrupted him and he had got the excitable professor back to his office, roared through his mind. But it was the expression on Stewart's face that plunged him into the depths.

He had been set up.

3

"God is not mocked," Armitage Shanks observed the day after the body of Izquierdo had been found in his office. He turned the little flask of his executive martini in its bed of ice, as if he were dialing in the deity.

"Now, now," Potts said.

"How did he die?"

"Alone. The way we all will." Not a favorite topic at the Old Bastards' table in the University Club. It was one thing to derive pleasure from the general collapse of higher education and of the culture at large since their own active years, but the destiny awaiting them all was best left implicit.

"He was strangled."

"I thought he was poisoned."

Potts glared at Wheeler. "Where did you hear that?"

"The same place you heard he was strangled."

Their understanding of what had happened to Izquierdo was pieced together from hearsay, the story in the local paper, and what they had heard from Debbie, the hostess. The club was abuzz with recent events, and Debbie picked up bits and pieces from the various tables and relayed it all to them.

"I think the provost hired a hit man," Potts said with a wicked grin.

"I never met the man," murmured Tasker, an emeritus professor of English and an infrequent presence at the table. Tasker could have passed unrecognized through the current ranks of his old department. Not to know is one thing, not to be known another. The waters of Lethe had closed over them all and, in lucid moments, they knew it.

"When was the last time a professor was found dead in his office?"

Here was a tangent they could all pursue, dredging up from memory the several incidents of those who had died with their boots on, something they had all once resolved to do, but in the end all had been more than content to enter the ranks of the retired, where at least they were known.

"They took someone from campus security in for questioning," Debbie told them, taking a chair and resting from her labors. These consisted in leading diners to their tables, giving them menus, and then returning to her desk just inside the door of the dining room to doodle. Once she had been a waitress, something only those at this table were likely to remember, and she kept her hand in, bringing their initial drinks, pouring coffee and water for them, from time to time sitting in on the wake they were holding for the past.

"What do you mean, took him in for questioning?"

"I'm only telling you what I heard."

"He must have been the hit man," Potts said.

"Maybe now they'll decide to tear down Decio," Shanks suggested.

"The donor's still alive."

So they were back to the doubtful future of the club. It was the consensus that the place would not be pulled down in their lifetime.

"The whole thing is a false alarm."

Debbie laughed. "Don't count on it."

"Well, you're pretty cheerful about the prospect."

"That's what you think."

"That's why I said."

"How did Izquierdo die?"

Debbie frowned. "Good Lord, you're ghoulish. They say he was strangled."

"By someone in campus security?"

"Who knows?"

"*¿Quién sabe?*" echoed Plaisance. Once his department had been called Romance languages; now it was modern languages. What might it not be tomorrow?

"*Panta rei.*"

"Who's he?"

"It's Greek, my dear fellow," Shanks said. "All things flow."

The translation had an adverse effect on a table full of old bladders. Most of the other diners had risen and gone. It was time for their own exodus from the dining room, the slow procession up the ramp for the handicapped and on to the men's room beyond. Armitage Shanks brought up the rear in every sense of the phrase and looked with melancholy at the procession of his fellow emeriti.

"I had not thought death had undone so many," he murmured.

4

Laura was on duty when a hysterical Pauline Izquierdo burst into the office of campus security, demanding to know what had happened to her husband.

"Oh my God! Haven't you heard?"

"Heard what? Tell me. No one will tell me anything."

She paced frantically from one side of the reception area to another. Laura picked up the phone and buzzed Crenshaw. She couldn't handle this any more than this woman could handle the news about her husband, whatever it was. Crenshaw did not answer. She knew he was in there. Others came into the reception area and immediately did a 180 and got out of there.

"That stupid Hector won't tell me. No one will tell me. They said to come here. Where is my husband?"

Not many women can retain their beauty while screaming hysterically, but Mrs. Izquierdo was an exception. Ringlets of hair pushed out of the black woolen cap she wore. Her ankle-length belted storm coat was of kelly green. Her eyes flashed; her voice ran up and down the scale of anguish. Laura was so fascinated that she almost stopped being angry at Crenshaw for hiding in his office.

"Come on," she said. She came around her desk, took the woman's hand, and pulled her down the hallway to Crenshaw's office. Of course the door was shut. Laura opened it and led the hysterical woman in. Crenshaw had been on his feet. He retreated to the window and looked with terror at the two women.

"Mrs. Izquierdo," Laura said. "No one has told her her husband has been murdered."

Laura pulled the door shut after her, then stood listening to the aria of anguish in Crenshaw's office. She hurried back to her desk to call Larry. What a day to call in sick.

Larry didn't answer the phone. Dark thoughts went through her mind. If he wasn't in his loft, where had he called from? Her phone rang and she snatched it up.

"Larry?"

"Get Detective Stewart out here," Crenshaw said in a strangled voice. Mrs. Izquierdo's wailing was twice audible, from down the hallway and, more piercingly, over the phone. "And you come in here. Now!"

Throughout the next half hour, Laura was registering everything in order to tell Larry. She managed to calm down Mrs. Izquierdo, more or less, but Crenshaw was determined to get the banshee out of there. No one downtown knew where Jimmy Stewart was.

"Laura will take you down there," Crenshaw said. "You shouldn't be alone."

Mrs. Izquierdo was in phase two of her confused grief. Laura got into her coat; Crenshaw actually helped her.

"Take my car," he urged, pressing the keys into her hands. Laura took them.

With relief in sight, Crenshaw in shirtsleeves helped her get the woman out to his car. There was a Hummer parked in the middle of the street, its motor still running.

"Who the hell put that there?" Crenshaw roared.

"That's mine."

"No problem. I'll take care of it."

When she was in the passenger seat, Crenshaw slammed the door and then stood there hugging himself with the stupidest expression on his stupid face. Laura started the car and, even before she left campus, turned on the siren. It was either that or face the woman's questions.

"You said he was murdered." She looked at Laura as if she had confessed to the crime.

"The police will explain everything."

"The police. You're the police."

Laura turned up the volume of the siren and with lights flashing sped downtown, ignoring the icy streets, liking it as cars pulled off to the side to let her through. There was a near miss as she tore through a red light when a car braked and then began to slide sideways through the intersection. Laura went into a slide herself but regained control. This had the effect of subduing her passenger.

When she pulled into the parking lot downtown, she had trouble bringing the car to a stop on the icy surface. It slid slowly into a snowbank and came to a halt, killing the motor. The siren kept going and she had trouble stopping it. When they got out of the car, Mrs. Izquierdo was more or less under control. Laura led her like a zombie inside.

"Homicide," she announced to the cop on duty. How did a fatso like that pass the physical? She pushed the thought away. "This is Mrs. Izquierdo, whose husband was found in his office on campus."

It was the new widow's cue to begin shrieking again. That was okay with Laura. She felt a bit like shrieking herself.

The next half hour or so was a confusing period. No one seemed to know of the murder on campus. Laura asked if they knew Detective Stewart. Of course they knew Detective Stewart. Well, this was his case, and this woman wanted someone in charge to tell her what had happened.

A tall man in a corduroy jacket with a Burberry coat over his arm, lining displayed, rose from a chair and became the voice of reason. He spoke soothingly to Mrs. Izquierdo; he stopped Laura when she headed for the door.

"Wait. I want to talk to you."

She waited. Finally the chief showed up. He knew less of what had happened than Mrs. Izquierdo, so Laura had to explain it to him, and to the man in the corduroy coat, while the horrified widow listened in.

"Where the hell is Stewart?" the chief demanded. "Get hold of Stewart."

Minions fled to carry out this order. The man in the corduroy jacket took Laura back to the reception area, got her seated, and brought her a cup of coffee. When he sat, he was holding a tablet. He licked the tip of his pencil.

"From the beginning."

All this was bearable because it was a story she was going to tell Larry. It was a strange interview, full of the oddest questions. Tell him all about Professor Izquierdo. Was he the campus atheist? Yes, yes, and the other day someone set his car afire. Her interviewer took this down eagerly.

The interview went on for twenty minutes, and Laura was more and more confused by the kind of questions she was being asked. Then the outside door opened and three men pushed through the revolving door. First, Jimmy Stewart, then Larry, and third, Philip Knight. Laura jumped to her feet.

"Larry!"

He stared at her and began to bawl like a baby. She took him in her arms. Stewart and Philip Knight shuffled and looked uncomfortable. Then Stewart asked what she was doing there.

"I brought Mrs. Izquierdo! No one had told her what happened."

"Ye gods."

"Laura," Larry said, burbling against her bosom. "They think I did it."

Stewart told Fatso to take Larry to a holding room so he could speak with Mrs. Izquierdo.

"Should I stay with him?"

"This officer will do that." He meant Laura.

When they were alone she coddled Larry as she often had, and he stopped whimpering. Honest to God, from a hysterical woman to a crying man. But this was Larry. He began to talk.

They had taken him to Decio. He thought they wanted his assistance. He looked at Laura and his mouth trembled. There, there. Then that creep in the office next to Izquierdo's recognized him from that night he had paid a visit to Izquierdo's office. Oscar Wack told them the whole story, which he seemed to think turned on planting a pogo stick in his office. He was sure Izquierdo had put them up to it, so he could be accused of God knows what.

"What did you tell them?"

"Nothing."

"You'll need a lawyer."

"Oh my God."

"Larry, what you did is not what they're after."

"They wanted to know why Wack spoke in the plural when he told the story. Of course he meant Henry."

"Did you tell them?"

"No! And don't you either."

"I think Henry should fess up."

"What good would that do?"

"Maybe you're right."

The door opened and the man in the corduroy coat came in and took a seat at the table. Larry stared at him. "Who are you?"

"Just tell it all in your own words. Have they charged you yet?"

They? "Who are you?"

The door opened again and Jimmy Stewart came in.

"What the hell are you doing here, Grafton?"

The corduroy jacket rose. "The public has a right to know, Stewart."

"Get out of here."

He got out of there. "Who is he?" Laura asked.

"Scoop Grafton. He calls himself a reporter. You can leave now. I want to talk to Larry."

"I'm part of it."

"What do you mean."

"I gave the master key for Decio to him."

Stewart slumped into a chair. "What did you tell Grafton?" He erased the question with an angry wave of his hand. "What the hell were you doing in Izquierdo's office?"

5

The local paper was full of Scoop Grafton's story; there were lengthy interviews with Laura and Larry, accompanied by what must have been the photographs taken when they joined Notre Dame security. Crenshaw said that both of them were on indefinite leave, pending a decision on their future employment. The campus papers, both those subsidized by student fees and the unsubsidized and independent, were full of the story. The campus was being described as a war zone in which cars were firebombed and dissidents murdered at their desks. Grateful students of Professor Izquierdo gave testimonials to his fearless attacks on Christianity. A girl who was writing her senior thesis on Feuerbach under Izquierdo's direction said that his course alone was reason enough for her having come to Notre Dame. As a rule, faculty dodged reporters. Those inclined to go on the record would doubtless submit op-ed essays. Hector, the departmental secretary, basked in the attention given him.

"He was one of the kindest men I ever knew." His eyes flashed as he said this, lest the reporter dare to contradict hm.

"What did his colleagues think of him?"

"What do you mean?"

"He was a maverick, wasn't he?"

"We are all mavericks here."

He was shut up after that. Wack had lodged a protest that the departmental secretary should presume to act as spokesman for them all.

"Would you like to?" McCerb, the chair, asked.

"Ha ha."

"Of course, there would be a conflict of interest in your case."

What did that mean? What had that catty Hector said? He consulted Lucy Goessen about it.

"I suppose they mean you'll be called as a witness. I imagine I will be, too."

"But I don't know anything!"

"I wouldn't make it that sweeping." But she smiled and patted his arm when she said it. Oscar purred. He was again certain that he and Lucy could become good friends. Not colleagues, friends.

■ ■ ■ ■

Larry Douglas's status was unclear. He was still being held for questioning, and his lawyer, a furtive fellow named Furlong, made a lengthy harangue about civil liberties, a phrase or two of which appeared in the newspaper accounts. On television, he was allowed to talk, but muted, while a voice-over explained what Furlong apparently wished to say. And then the scarf was found in Larry's loft.

It must have been five feet long, gaudy, striped. It was immediately recognized as Izquierdo's. It seemed twisted. It was rushed to the lab; results were collated with the coroner's report. It seemed that the murder weapon had been found.

"What did Larry say when you told him?" Roger asked. Jimmy Stewart and Phil were discussing this latest event in the Knight apartment. Father Carmody had been invited, but the continuing arctic weather had prevented it.

"The kid is almost catatonic."

Fauxhall, an assistant prosecutor, was trying to get Jimmy to sign on to a scenario. It is known that Larry was able to enter Izquierdo's office at will, thanks to the master key filched from campus security. Having established this, he bides his time. One night, while Izquierdo is still in his office, Larry enters. Imagine how surprised the professor must have been. But Larry would have been wearing his uniform. Some specious excuse must have been given. The scarf, with the professor's other wraps, is hung on a stand in the corner behind the desk. Did Larry marvel at the scarf of many colors, want to examine it more closely? Now he is behind the desk, he has the scarf, he loops it over the head of the still unsuspecting professor and begins to twist. There are signs of the struggle Izquierdo put up, kicking like crazy against the dying of the light. The desk itself is moved in the struggle. And then resistance ends. Larry removes the scarf, pushes the desk back approximately to where it had been, and leaves.

"Conveniently keeping the scarf in his loft so it could be found."

"I needn't tell you of the inconsistency of the criminal mind." Fauxhall might have already been addressing a jury. "Well, what do you think?"

"Even Furlong could make mincemeat out of that."

But it was Mrs. Izquierdo who did. She telephoned Jimmy.

"That is not Raul's scarf."

"Why do you say that?"

"Because it's here, hanging in the hall closet."

Jimmy went out to the house and looked at the scarf, identical to the one that had been found in Larry's loft.

"It's been here all along?"

"Of course it has."

"Where did he buy it?"

"I bought it for him."

From Whistler's, a men's store in the mall. The salesman took Jimmy to Whistler's office. When he learned the purpose of the visit, he wasn't sure he wanted his establishment mixed up in this.

"It already is."

"I am not responsible for what happens to items I sell."

"Of course you're not. Let's talk about this scarf." Jimmy had with him the scarf Pauline Izquierdo had given him. Whistler reached for it, then withdrew his hand.

"How many of these do you suppose you've sold?"

"I'm surprised I sold any."

"I see what you mean."

Whistler kept records, of course, and he

found proof of Mrs. Izquierdo's purchase, but of no other. There had been three such scarves in his inventory. The scarf found in Larry's loft had Whistler's tag in it. The explanation seemed to be that it had been on a discount table with dozens of other items that had not sold well. No record would have been kept of such a purchase, only a generic "special sale" designation.

"So who is trying to frame Larry Douglas?"

"When we know that, we will know who strangled Izquierdo."

Roger sat humming and shaking his head. "If I killed someone, I would want to get rid of the murder instrument rather than plant it somewhere."

"I needn't tell you of the inconsistency of the criminal mind." Jimmy crossed his fingers when he said it.

"And what of the plastic bag containing pages of *Via Media,* scissors, glue?"

Jimmy shrugged. No prints, but the pages had been compared with uncut pages of the paper, and it seemed pretty certain that the contents of the bag explained the threatening letters that had caused such interest some weeks before.

"None of those threats were actually carried out, were they?"

Phil suggested that, since they had been a spoof, they could have been sent by Izquierdo. Particularly since one of the addressees was the colleague he loathed.

"Oscar Wack." What interested Roger was Wack's assumption that Larry had not been alone the night he had surprised him in Izquierdo's office.

"That woman insists she was with him," Jimmy said.

"But waiting outside."

"So she says."

"Wack says he saw three people riding away in a golf cart."

"The third man."

Phil began to give an impression of the theme song of that old movie.

"I'd talk with Laura again if I were you," Roger said.

But first Jimmy talked to Larry. He had been released when Mrs. Izquierdo produced her husband's scarf. It had been assumed that the scarf found in Larry's loft had been the murder weapon, but the lab told the deflated Fauxhall that it could have been the other scarf. The marks made on the throat of Izquierdo pointed to such a scarf, but there was nothing on either scarf to enable them to decide which had been the murder weapon. And what else did they have?

"I'm still on leave," Larry complained. "Crenshaw let Laura come back to work, but I am still on indefinite leave."

Furlong, Larry's lawyer, had transferred his energies to combating the injustice with which campus security was treating his client. Furlong was a Democrat and thus despised the present occupant of the White House, but he argued passionately that providing security for a community often required unusual means. Larry was a zealous young man, his actions had been unusual, but his motives were clear. Furlong himself wasn't clear on what those motives were, but no matter. He had been given lengthy coverage in campus newspapers, editors being delighted to criticize the administration through a third party.

"Who was with you the night you entered Izquierdo's office?"

"Laura."

"Who was the third person?"

"What third person?"

"Professor Wack says he saw three people ride away in the golf cart."

"I don't know what he's talking about."

"He must be a great friend of yours."

"Who?"

"The third man who didn't come forward in your defense."

Larry just stared at him. Laura was no more help, but again Jimmy felt he was not getting the full story. So he began to keep tabs on the young couple. It turned out that Kimberley who worked in the coroner's office knew Larry. Feeley remembered that his assistant had gone out with the young man. So Jimmy talked with her.

"Oh yes," she said. "We went out a few times. We shared an interest in poetry."

"Ah."

"But that's all it was."

It turned out that she was now going with someone else in campus security, Henry Grabowski. Not that she volunteered this, but following her around for a few days brought this to the surface. Was Henry the third man?

Crenshaw began to shake his head as soon as Jimmy brought up the subject.

"You know I can't give out information like that."

"You don't have to, of course. It must be a pain in the neck having someone like Furlong on your case. I'd hate to get a court order and multiply your problems."

"A court order!"

"We've got a murder on your campus,

Crenshaw. An unsolved case. I need to pursue what leads I get. Why are you covering up for Henry Grabowski?"

"Covering up? He works here. You know that, I know that, everybody knows that."

Finally Crenshaw let Jimmy see Henry's application. Among the letters of recommendation was one from a teacher at St. Joe High School, Masterson, who happened to be Jimmy's brother-in-law. They had more or less avoided one another since Hazel left him, but that was only because they were no longer comfortable together. Jimmy called him up and invited him for a beer at Leaky's near the courthouse.

"Bat, how are you? Take a pew."

Masterson smiled and slid into the booth across from Jimmy. "You're the only one who calls me that."

"What do your students call you?"

"Sir."

"Remember a kid named Henry Grabowski?"

"Of course I do. Why do you ask?"

"He's been taken on by Notre Dame security."

Bat's beer had come, and he made a face before drinking. "What a waste."

"How do you mean?"

Bat told him about Henry's record as a

student, something Jimmy already knew, thanks to Crenshaw.

"He couldn't afford college?"

"He was a shoo-in for a fellowship, and there are loans. But it was Notre Dame or nothing. He wouldn't listen to me."

"Did he apply?"

"And was turned down. I told him thousands of applicants are turned down every year by Notre Dame. Tens of thousands. I suggested the route through Holy Cross College."

"Was he bitter or what?"

"All his life he had dreamt of going to Notre Dame."

"Well, he ended up there."

Bat shook his head and said again, "What a waste."

Professor Wack looked at the photograph Jimmy gave him. "Is he the man who was with Larry Douglas the night you surprised them in Izquierdo's office?"

"I didn't see him. I told you that. But I know this fellow. He and Izquierdo were thick as thieves."

"What do you mean?"

"He was up here a lot. I think Izquierdo was trying to tutor him. Raul wasn't all bad, you know."

Lucy Goessen also remembered seeing Henry when he came to see Izquierdo. "Raul said he was smarter than most of his students."

6

Kimberley was reluctant to show him around the morgue, but Henry kept after her. What was a girl like that doing working in a place like this? Feeley, the coroner, was another surprise.

"How did you end up here?" Henry asked.

"It's a long story."

"I'm listening."

It seemed almost noble that Feeley had abandoned all his dreams in order to keep his father on the local political payroll. It made them seem kindred spirits, in a way. "Did you ever read 'Winter Dreams' by Fitzgerald?"

Feeley just looked at him. But Kimberley knew the story.

Stealing Kimberley away from Larry Douglas had not been much of a triumph. Henry soon tired of her sentimental response to what she read.

"You should read Nietzsche."

"Maybe I will."

She tried *Zarathustra* but didn't like it. So he told her what Jeeves had said to Bertie Wooster. "You would not like Nietzsche, sir. He is fundamentally unsound." Kimberley began to remind Henry of one of Bertie's girlfriends.

"I think Wodehouse is silly."

"Of course he is."

"So why read him?"

"For the silliness."

"Now you're being silly."

"That's because you think I think what I say is true."

But there was no point in trying out Izquierdo's nihilism on her. A limited mind. Pretty as a picture, of course, there was no doubt of that. Henry's trouble was that the future had ceased to interest him. Once his whole life had been aimed at becoming a student at Notre Dame. That would have put him on the one track he wanted. Meeting with Izquierdo was a poor substitute, but then it led nowhere, so that became its attraction. If he had been a real student, getting a high grade would have entered into it, but all he got from Izquierdo was the endorsement of his sense of superiority, and that only added to the bitterness of his disappointment. Putting the torch to Izquierdo's Corvette was an instance of what Izquierdo called an *acte gratuite.* Motiveless. Done in order to do it. And to get a rise out of Izquierdo. Raul's reaction was a disappointment. So one night he went to Decio and put the plastic bag with the cuttings and scissors and glue he had used in fashioning those threatening letters in a drawer in Izquierdo's desk.

When he heard someone outside the door, he quickly turned off the office light and sat as still as he could in Izquierdo's chair. A key in the lock. He prepared himself to greet Izquierdo, searching desperately for an explanation he might give of being here, and then he was looking into the terrified face of Larry Douglas.

For days now he had been mystified by Larry's silence about that night when they took him in for questioning. Henry had thought of going downtown and asking to see Larry, he had thought of quizzing Laura about it, but he didn't do the first, and Laura was suspended along with Larry.

Henry tried various explanations. Larry had told them that he had found Henry already in Izquierdo's office and they were keeping it quiet. Maybe he was under surveillance. The best response to that was to put Detective Stewart under surveillance.

He called in sick, asking for Crenshaw.

"I've got the flu."

"Everybody's got the flu."

"I can't come to work."

"You better not. I don't want to catch it."

So Henry followed Stewart around. He watched him enter Whistler's and knew the reason. But who would remember buying a scarf from a table of discounted items? When Henry had seen the duplicate of Izquierdo's scarf — actually there were two on the table — he asked his mom to buy it for him. She did, but she thought it was ridiculous.

Nothing happened after Stewart's trip to the mall. Henry feared that his mother would be questioned about the scarf, but nothing happened. Henry breathed a little easier. When Stewart spent an evening at the Knights' apartment, Henry decided that the time had come for him to get a new faculty mentor. He found out where Roger Knight's class was held and asked if he could sit in. Knight just assumed he was a student.

"So what did you think?" Roger Knight asked him afterward. He had been surrounded by students after the class, but Henry had waited for him by his golf cart.

"F. Marion Crawford?"

"Have you ever read him?"

"On my list, he comes right after Winston Churchill. The other one."

Roger's popularity was a mystery to Henry. He could understand that women students would feel motherly toward a man that helpless, shaped like a balloon, getting around a real effort. But his mind was too elusive for Henry, and allusive. He realized that Izquierdo had flattered him even while being condescending. Roger with his big blue-eyed baby stare could have talked rings around Izquierdo. What hadn't the guy read? But it was the simplicity of his religious faith that marked him. After Izquierdo, this was a real switch. Then Roger surprised him by saying he had heard Henry was a protégé of the campus atheist.

"Protégé?"

"I'm told you often visited his office."

"Only in daytime hours," Henry said, then wished he hadn't. For the matter of that, he wished he hadn't looked up Roger Knight. Of course Roger would know everything his brother knew and his brother everything that Stewart did. Henry felt a sudden impulse to talk to Roger, to ask his help, but he fought it.

Someone was playing him for a fool, and

he just couldn't believe it was Larry Douglas. Why was he keeping quiet? The discovery of that scarf in Larry's loft should have turned him into a babbling cooperative witness, but even then, nothing.

It had to do with Kimberley, that must be it. He was too proud to point a finger at the guy who had walked off with his girl.

At home he went up to his room, telling his mom he would be right down for supper, but he had to check something first. He opened his dresser drawer, pushed aside the neat pile of Hanes shorts, and pulled out the many-colored scarf. It was still here. It had always been here. So who had tossed an identical scarf into Larry's loft? How many of them were there?

7

When young Father Conway was asked to speak to the widow of Professor Izquierdo, he welcomed this opportunity for pastoral work. He hadn't endured all those years of study in order to occupy an office in the Main Building. Not that he thought this would be easy.

First, he made sure he had all the information about the late professor, and of course he was briefed by the university lawyer. That was when it dawned on Tim Conway that, for some, the main concern was that the widow would sue the university. So in some ways, he was engaged in making a preemptive strike. In his own mind, he was calling on her in his capacity as a priest. His lips moved in prayer as he drove. Please grant me the grace to say the right, the healing thing.

"Pauline," she said when he had addressed her twice as Mrs. Izquierdo.

"Tim."

"Oh, I couldn't call you Tim, Father."

"That's perfectly all right." There were laypeople like that, insistent on the dignity of the priesthood, sticklers for protocol and etiquette.

She said, "My father's name was Tim."

She was a woman of striking good looks, even a celibate could appreciate that. Dark hair with threads of gray, actually white, providing an intriguing contrast.

"Have arrangements been made?"

"Arrangements? Oh. The body is still at the morgue. There will be a cremation, that's what he would have wanted. You know he was an atheist."

"We will hold a memorial service in any case."

She surprised him by smiling. "If you think it will help."

"The university intends to give you all the help it can."

She nodded, waiting for him to go on. So he took a folder from his briefcase and outlined what the university felt, in these extraordinary circumstances, it could do to alleviate her sorrow.

"And there is of course the amount that accrued in his retirement fund."

"Maybe I'll stop working."

He felt like an insurance agent, not a priest, and she baffled him. From what he had heard of her reaction when she learned of her husband's death, Tim had steeled himself for hysterics, anger, accusations, whatever. Instead she sat on her couch with the flowing, florid housecoat dramatically draped around her and reaching to the floor, the picture of composure. He realized she was barefoot. Until they had sat, her feet were concealed by the garment she wore.

"I know it's difficult to speak of these things."

She shook her head. "I've had time to think, Father. Ours was what Raul called an open marriage." A little smile. "Meaning he could cheat on me."

"Did he?"

"He was a man."

"Well." He looked at the picture behind her. *The Temptation of St. Anthony.* "There are no children?"

"By me? No. We were too selfish for that."

"What about you? Your husband was an atheist . . ."

"Who every day recited the prayer to his guardian angel." She lifted her eyes and joined her hands. " 'Angel of God, my guardian dear, to whom God's love entrusts me here, ever this day be at my side, to light and guard, to rule and guide.' "

"An atheist who prayed?"

"He was a bundle of contradictions. Maybe we all are."

"So he was raised Catholic?"

"We were married in the Church. The atheism came later."

"And you?"

"Have I lost my faith? I don't know. I don't think so."

"Well, we can talk of that later."

"Will they find the one who did it?"

He couldn't say. He supposed so. It was unthinkable that a professor could be killed in his office and the murderer go undiscovered. Did she have any suspicions?

"I'm glad I told the police about the scarf. I was certain that young man hadn't done it, and then I found Raul's scarf." She smiled. "Actually I thought the man they had arrested was someone else."

"Oh?"

"Someone Raul was tutoring. Also in campus security."

"You've had to discuss all this with the police?"

"They've been very nice. Very considerate."

"Good."

Her eyes drifted away. "Our parents were so happy when Raul was hired by Notre Dame. So were we." She looked at him and her eyes seemed moist. "Beware of answered prayers. Isn't that what they say?"

"I'll say a Mass for the repose of his soul."

"He wasn't sure he had one."

"Of course he did." It was all he had now.

Again she smiled. She made him feel younger than he was. He repeated for her what the university offered to do for her, and she listened carefully, and again he reminded her that her husband would have accrued a goodly sum in his retirement account.

"And there is insurance."

"Ah. Our substitute for providence. I'm quoting Raul."

He supposed it must be some consolation to know that she would be very comfortable, economically. There was also insurance on the car that had been burned.

"I noticed the Hummer in the driveway."

"That's mine."

"I've never ridden in one."

"It gives a sense of power."

A silence fell, and he didn't know how to break it. A sense of his own inadequacy swept over him. He began to gather together his papers and put them in his briefcase.

"I should have offered you coffee."

"I've had my cup for the day."

"Just one."

He nodded and rose. "Well, I'll keep in touch."

"Thanks for coming, Tim."

He thought of that farewell as he slipped and slid down the driveway to his car parked behind a drift beside the suburban street. He had four sisters, but that hadn't helped him figure out Pauline Izquierdo.

When he got back to campus, he stopped by Roger Knight's apartment and was glad to find the Huneker Professor of Catholic Studies in. He wanted to talk about his visit to Mrs. Izquierdo with Roger before returning to the provost's office.

8

Young Father Conway could not believe
that Roger had never been to Rome. The
enormous professor spoke of the city as if
he had spent years there, and he could hold
forth on the way Rome was a palimpsest —
Tim looked it up later — with the Etruscan
past under the republic and empire, over
which the medieval and Renaissance had
been laid.

"How I envy you, Father, four years
there."

But Roger knew that Tim Conway had not
dropped by in order to talk about his
student years in the Eternal City, so he
stopped praising F. Marion Crawford's two-
volume history of Rome and busied himself
making hot chocolate.

"I've just come from Mrs. Izquierdo."

"Can you tell me about it?" Roger had
turned and looked eagerly at the young
priest.

"I don't see why not."

"Good, good."

And so they sat and Father Conway spoke of his chat with the widow of Professor Izquierdo. An atheist who prayed.

"She said theirs was an open marriage."

"Open to adultery?"

"On his part anyway. She was very blasé about it. I had expected a hysterical woman, but not at all. Not that I know what the behavior of a wife whose husband has been murdered ought to be."

The account of the scarf got Roger's whole attention. It had been a lucky day for Larry Douglas when Mrs. Izquierdo informed the police that her husband's scarf was in the closet of their home.

"And now there are two."

"She said she was sure that young man hadn't killed her husband. Funny thing, though. She had mistaken him for someone else in campus security."

"She said that?"

"Well, in any case, there was the scarf."

Roger did not press the young priest. They sipped their cocoa, and then they were talking about the terrible weather, so the visit was coming to an end.

After Father Conway left, Roger went back to his study, settled himself in his special chair, and thought about the strange events of the past weeks.

Threatening notes had been received by the provost, the dean of Arts and Letters, the football coach, and Oscar Wack. The discovery of that plastic bag in Izquierdo's desk indicated that Izquierdo had fashioned those letters. Given his relations with Wack, it made sense that his loathsome colleague would receive one. Then there had been the strange episode of the burning wastebasket, allegedly the work of Wack, but who knew? Next had come the burning of Izquierdo's car and then the discovery of his dead body at his desk in his Decio office.

But before that, Larry Douglas had paid a clandestine visit to Izquierdo's office, only to be surprised by the ubiquitous Wack.

"What reason did he give for being there?"

"According to Jimmy, Douglas says he was investigating the burning of the car."

"What did he expect to find?"

Phil shrugged. "He didn't know. Maybe a threatening note."

But it was Wack's claim that Larry had not been alone in Izquierdo's office that night that interested Jimmy Stewart. It interested Roger, too, however slender a reed Wack was to lean on.

"He didn't see who it was?"

"Larry prevented that. They went into Wack's office to talk."

"And the pogo stick?"

"Larry says he doesn't know anything about that."

"Yet it belonged to Izquierdo and was found in Wack's office."

Wack's insistence that, from his window, he had seen three people drive away from Decio in the golf cart confirmed Jimmy's belief that there was a third man.

And neither Larry nor Laura would say who it was. Or admit that there was a third man.

"It had to be Henry Grabowski," Jimmy said.

"He sat in on my class," Roger said.

"Maybe you ought to pursue it," Jimmy said.

"He seems to be a brilliant young man."

"So what's he doing in campus security?"

"What are you doing on the police force?"

"I'm not a brilliant young man."

But Henry Grabowski didn't return to Roger's class.

9

Larry's leave of absence had been terminated, and he was back to work. Relieved as he was, it was as if he had been delivered over to Laura. Oh, she had stuck by him, she had been there when he needed someone, but that didn't mean he wanted to get back in the old rut. She thought he was nuts to keep Henry's name out of it.

"What would be the point of mentioning it?"

It was clear she didn't know. But Larry would never forget that Henry had already been in Izquierdo's office that night when he went to Decio with the master key. Larry had had time to think about that when he was under suspicion. He knew he hadn't killed Izquierdo, and he knew that whoever did had access to his office. An idea was born. Now that he was cleared, he was going to solve this case. He could never forget the elation he had felt when Detective Stewart had called and asked if he could be of help in the investigation. Only to find that what Jimmy wanted was to learn if Wack could place him as the nighttime visitor to Izquierdo's office. What a crushing letdown that had been. Even so, he was professional enough to appreciate what Jimmy Stewart had done.

So it had been important to convince Laura that mentioning Henry's being there that night was simply irrelevant. Irrelevant, hell. How had he gotten into the office? And what was he doing there anyway? Larry's story was that he had been in search of clues to the burning of Izquierdo's car. Henry said the same. But the way Henry had been dressed, all in black, like someone out of *The Pink Panther*.

Had Henry killed Izquierdo? It was one thing to ask himself that when he was stewing downtown with that nut Furlong assuring him that they would beat this rap, but when he was with Henry again he found it hard to think that the guy could have done such a thing. It was the way that scarf had shown up in his loft that kept Larry on the trail. There was something screwy about Henry, smart as he no doubt was. And he was happy to talk about his sessions with Izquierdo.

"It was like a tutorial. I would read books and we would discuss them."

"Why?"

"All men by nature desire to know. Aristotle."

"Sure. But why would he give you all that free time?"

"He wanted to corrupt youth."

"How is Kimberley?"

Henry chuckled. "You can have her back, buddy. A great package, but it's empty."

Empty! What had drawn Larry to Kimberley was her love of poetry. She had been the first person he had been able to speak with about the poets he loved. Imagine discussing poetry with Laura. Well, maybe Angelou.

He didn't dignify Henry's magnanimous offer with a reply. Kimberley had liked him before she even heard of Henry Grabowski. Larry was certain if they could just be alone and talk about, say, Richard Wilbur's poetry, or Dana Gioia's, all would be well. The difficulty was getting free of Laura. A difficulty doubled because he did not want her hanging around while he checked out Henry.

Where to begin? He remembered that ignominious scene in Decio when Wack had brought that stupid pogo stick out of his office, as if that was the point of bringing

Larry up there. Not that the pogo stick wasn't a mystery. Then Larry had a distracting thought. What about Wack? The guy seemed to haunt the third floor of Decio; what had he been doing lurking in his office that night? And hadn't Izquierdo accused him of setting his wastebasket on fire? If a wastebasket, why not a Corvette? The more he thought about it, the more Henry faded from the picture and that creepy little Wack took center stage.

It was not an easy matter getting around campus on a bicycle in this kind of weather. He and Henry started off together, heading south from campus security, but Henry swung off to the right. Larry let him go, but then he doubled back and followed him. Henry locked his bike outside the Huddle and went inside. So that was his idea of being on duty. Disgusted, Larry set out for his original destination, Decio. As he pedaled, he remembered the woman professor, Goessen, illustrating the use of the pogo stick as Larry was led away by Stewart and Philip Knight.

When he came out of the elevator on the third floor, he thought of knocking on Professor Goessen's door, but he didn't know what he would say to her. So he continued on and knocked on Wack's door.

"Who is it?"

He knocked again, and again Wack spoke from behind the closed door, asking who it was. Larry waited.

The door opened and Wack stared at him. Larry had opened his coat so that his uniform was visible.

"What do you want?"

"Just a few questions."

Larry went in, with Wack moving backward, keeping the door between him and Larry. Larry took a chair and brought out a notebook.

"I have nothing to say to you."

"Let's start with that pogo stick. When did you remove it from Izquierdo's office?"

"Remove it? You put it here!"

It was hard to tell with a guy this excitable, but Wack appeared to be telling the truth. He decided to sit behind his desk.

"Okay. Then this is the mystery. You didn't take it from Izquierdo's office, and I sure as hell didn't put it here. So who did?"

"This is preposterous."

"If not you or me, someone else. Do you have any idea?"

Wack gave it some thought, grudgingly. "You're just trying to exonerate yourself."

"Oh come on. In itself, this is no big deal. A pogo stick. Even if it had been you or

242

me, it's not a federal offense. Still, you and I will want to know who did it." He paused. "It could be connected with something that is serious. Like Izquierdo's death."

Larry was enjoying this. Every time Wack spoke, he scribbled in his notebook.

"You must suspect someone. Has there been anyone, any stranger, lurking around this floor?"

"Oh, Izquierdo held open house. He didn't care how distracting it is to have students coming and going all the time. Or nonstudents, for that matter."

"Like?"

"You must know him. He works in campus security, too."

"Grabowski."

"I don't know his name, but he was up here several times a week."

No doubt while on duty.

"You never talked to him?"

"Well, I went over there several times and asked them to keep it low. I do most of my research right here."

"You're here a lot."

Wack just tossed his hair.

"When was the last time Grabowski was here?"

Wack couldn't remember. "I think Izquierdo gave him a key. Some professors let favorite students use their offices."

"He could have let himself in?"

"If he had a key."

This was going nowhere. Larry closed his notebook. "Well, I guess that's it for now."

"For now? This is harassment. If you come back, I will call your superior."

Larry pulled the door shut behind him. As he did, a door across the hall opened and Professor Goessen came out. Larry gave her a salute and she smiled.

"I thought they arrested you," she said.

"Mistaken identity."

"Who were they after, the other one?"

"What other one?"

"He wore a uniform, too."

"That's so we can't be told apart. You were pretty impressive on that pogo stick."

She laughed. "It's a knack you don't forget. Like riding a bicycle."

They went down in the elevator together. At the entrance, she bundled up. "Oh, this ungodly weather. And I had an offer from Florida State."

She pushed through the door, lowered her head, and started for the library. Larry's bicycle was not where he had left it. He looked all over for the darned thing. Henry. It had to be Henry. But why? He started off for campus security, not liking the prospect of reporting his bike had been stolen.

10

The after-class discussion was short — because of the weather, everyone wanted to get back to his room — and Roger walked carefully out to his golf cart. Henry Grabowski was sitting behind the wheel. He gave Roger a salute.

"Got the key?"

Roger slid onto the seat and handed Henry the key. He turned it and depressed the pedal, and they moved off.

"I have to talk to you."

"You know where I live."

Henry shook his head. "Let's go to your office."

"You know where it is?"

Henry hesitated, then said, "Give me directions."

Brownson Hall is behind Sacred Heart Basilica, as old a building as there is on campus, and one that had been put to many uses since it ceased being the convent of the nuns who had done the baking and cooking in the early days. The lower wing now contained offices for various auxiliary and supernumerary teachers, the lower rungs of the academic ladder. Roger's office was there because he could park in the lot next to the building, from which access to the building was easy for him. Roger hadn't been in the office for a week or more, because of the weather.

Henry drove without talking, carefully guiding the electric cart along the shoveled walks, avoiding students who walked along in a frozen trance. He didn't need directions.

When he had parked in the lot next to Brownson, Henry waited for Roger to ease himself out, then took his arm and led him to the entrance.

"I feel that I'm in custody."

"So do I."

Roger had to unbutton his jacket to try several pockets, looking for his keys. They had been in a jacket pocket all along. He let them in, switching on the light as he squeezed himself through the narrow door.

Four walls of bookshelves, the overflow of his library, which continued to overflow as he made new purchases. Phil often asked him to weed out things he didn't need, but

Roger would not have known where to begin. How do you know when you will need a book again? He hung up his great hooded outer garment, went around the desk, and sank with a sigh into his chair. He looked receptively at Henry, who sat opposite him, having dropped his jacket on the floor.

"They think I did it."

Roger smiled. "Who is 'they' and what is 'it'?"

"Stewart is investigating me. I know it. Your brother works with him, and I suppose he tells you everything."

"So we're talking about Raul Izquierdo?"

"I didn't kill him."

"Has anyone accused you?"

"Don't." His voice almost broke. "They will. Someone is trying to set me up."

The office was pleasantly warm, but Roger rubbed his hands, still a little numb from the cold. "Tell me about Izquierdo. I never knew him."

"I did. He gave me a lot of his time."

"In his office?"

Henry nodded. "We went through the books on his syllabus."

"What course was that?"

"It was called Criticism. There was a motto on the first page of the syllabus.

'Nothing is but what is not.' "

"Shakespeare."

"Is it? He hated Shakespeare."

"That's hard to believe."

"I think he hated literature."

"Tell me about your discussions."

"We pretty well settled down to Nietzsche. The works themselves. Some secondary stuff. There's a book, *Zarathustra's Secret*—"

"Kohler."

"You know it?"

"An odd book. But then Nietzsche was an odd man."

"So was Izquierdo."

"You were going to tell me about him."

After Henry began, Roger wanted to stop him, but he doubted that he could have. This was why Henry had waited for him and come to his office. His admiration for Izquierdo had turned to hatred.

"There was something diabolical about him. It wasn't just the delight he took in shaking the faith of students. He was a predator. Students, colleagues. He told me that he and his wife had an agreement. Maybe he just meant that she knew what he was up to. She certainly didn't approve."

Once when Henry was in Izquierdo's office talking with the professor, Mrs. Izquierdo burst in without warning. "She seemed disappointed to find me there."

So Henry had been introduced to Mrs. Izquierdo, and then she got in touch with him.

"She wanted to quiz me about her husband. She actually asked me to spy on him."

"And?"

Henry inhaled. "I fed her a lot of stories, made up, what she wanted to hear. I told myself it was the sort of thing Izquierdo would do. Anyhow, it wasn't much fun after that, talking about books."

"Why aren't you a student?"

"It's a long story."

Roger opened his hands. "I'd like to hear it."

It was the fact that Henry's mother worked on campus, a member of the crew that cleaned student rooms, that seemed most poignant to Roger. Her long employment might have lowered Henry's tuition, if he had been admitted. But he had been turned down.

"There are other universities."

Henry shook his head. He had defined his future so narrowly, alternatives were out of the question.

"What a disappointment that must have been."

"To put it mildly."

"Yet you took a job here."

"That was stupid. I wanted to be here and look at the students and tell myself I was as good as any of them, maybe better. So I became a freelance student. You let me sit in your class? Most of the time I did that without asking. I was flattered when Izquierdo took an interest in me."

"Not many professors would have been so generous with their time."

"Oh, it wasn't generosity. He wanted a disciple. I guess he got one in a sense."

After Mrs. Izquierdo burst in on them, the tutorials became sessions in which Henry became the unwilling confidante of Izquierdo's marital woes.

"He would quote Prince Andre to Pierre. Never marry."

Henry fell silent. He looked around the room, then over Roger's head.

"Now comes the worst part."

Izquierdo had urged Henry to seduce his wife.

Another long silence. Roger waited.

The office seemed to have become a confessional of the newer sort, penitent facing the confessor, trying not to make what he had done seem less awful than it was. Henry had fallen in with the scheme. His entree was to go to Mrs. Izquierdo and tell her, as if in shock, that her husband was carrying on an affair with Professor Goessen.

"She believed me. I believed myself. Maybe it was true. At first she was angry at me, kill the messenger, but then she started to cry, and . . ."

And he had taken the older woman in his arms, he had brushed away her tears, he had murmured a line of Swinburne.

"Then she laughed and pushed me away. Her laughing cleared the air. She made coffee and we sat and she told me what a bastard she had married. I already knew that."

She asked if her husband had sent him to her. He denied it but didn't think she believed him. The question put him in a light that alarmed him. What had he become?

"That's when I set fire to his car."

Henry waited for Roger to express shock, but Roger only nodded.

"The fire in his wastebasket suggested it to me. That and the threatening letters."

"Tell me about those."

"We composed them. I delivered them, the invisible messenger in his campus security uniform. He delivered the one to

Wack himself, slipped it under his door. What a pair."

In the parking lot outside the window, car engines were starting up. It had grown dark, an early winter evening.

"Why did you and Larry Douglas go to his office that night?"

Henry smiled. "I was already there when Larry showed up. I don't know which of us was more scared when he came in and saw me."

"You were already there?"

"Izquierdo had given me a key. He told me I could use the office whenever he wasn't there. The idea was that in the evening it would be free."

"You went there often?"

"At first, when I was still impressed by him."

"You were just there working when Larry showed up."

Henry shook his head. "I was trying to figure out some way to really shake him. I thought his Corvette going up in flames would do it, but he was almost calm. He was sure his wife had done it."

"I can understand why you are worried."

He had a key to the office; he had come to loathe Izquierdo, feeling he had turned him into a monster like himself. Of course that would be considered motive enough to kill the man.

"I didn't do it."

But which "I" hadn't done it? It is all too easy for us to separate ourselves from our deeds. Augustine had developed that in the *Confessions*. The telephone rang and they both stared at it. Seven rings and then it stopped.

"That will be my brother, wondering where I am."

"Tell me what to do."

"Come home with me and have supper."

"I'll have to call my mom."

Roger pushed the phone toward him. He swung away while Henry talked to his mother. How his voice changed, softer, gentle. Then a long silence before he hung up.

"Stewart has been there. With a warrant."

As he got into his hooded outer garment, Roger said, "What I don't understand is the scarves."

"Neither do I."

Phil was waiting anxiously when Roger came in. "I've brought a guest."

"Jimmy's coming." Phil's tone told Roger that something was up.

In the kitchen, Roger donned his baseball

cap and wrapped himself in a huge apron and put water on for pasta.

"There's beer in the icebox."

"I don't drink."

"Neither do I."

"That's more for me," Phil said, trying to sound cheerful.

Roger had already dished up when Jimmy Stewart came. He tried not to look surprised when he saw Henry Grabowski at the table. But he waited until they were finished, and the dishes taken away.

"I've been to your house," Jimmy said to Henry.

"My mom told me."

"With a warrant. You're in trouble, son."

Henry looked at Roger as if everything he had told him could help him now.

"I found this scarf in your drawer. Want to tell me about that?"

"My mom bought it for me."

"Now we have three of the damned things."

"Maybe I will have a beer."

Henry got up, started toward the kitchen, then dashed for the outer door, pulling it open and rushing outside. It took quite a struggle before Phil and Jimmy subdued him. Roger, still wearing his baseball cap and apron, brought Henry his jacket. The boy looked desolately at him when he was put in the backseat of Jimmy's prowler. Phil got in beside him. Roger stood in the snow watching the red taillights disappear into the night.

PART FOUR

1

The case against Henry Grabowski was, as had been that against Larry Douglas, circumstantial — only there were more circumstances. In Larry's case, it had been the fact that he had surreptitiously gained entry to Izquierdo's office, plus the scarf found in his room and thought to be the murder weapon. Mrs. Izquierdo's production of the identical scarf from the hall closet in the Izquierdo home led to the release of Larry, to the disappointment of Fauxhall, the deputy prosecutor, and to the relief of Jimmy Stewart. Jimmy had never been able to convince himself that Larry could have done such a thing. He was having a similar problem with Henry.

Listening to Jimmy and Phil discuss the arrest, Roger was of two minds as to whether he ought to tell them things that he knew only because Henry had confided in him. Of those things, the most significant was Henry's claim that he had set fire to Iz-quierdo's Corvette. At the moment, that seemed only slightly more important than the fire that had been set in Izquierdo's wastebasket, except of course that it sug-gested something more than a mild dislike for Henry's quondam mentor.

It was the testimony of Oscar Wack that Henry was a frequent visitor to Izquierdo's office, and Henry's own admission that he had a key to the office and had been told he might use it when the professor was not in, that weighed heavily against Henry.

"How often did you go there?"

"For a while, it was several times a week."

"During the day?"

"No. He would be there during the day." Henry made a face. "And of course I work."

"So it was only at night that you used the office."

"During the day, when I went, it was for tutoring. That's what we called it."

"You're a student?"

"I work in campus security." There was a bitter edge to his voice.

"It sounds to me that you were working more than any student."

"But less than a cop?"

Jimmy found him a smart-ass, but he liked him. Larry Douglas was the kind of eager beaver it was hard not to like, whereas Henry made it tough. But Jimmy had talked with Bat Masterson, and he knew the lifelong dream that had been smashed when Henry had not been admitted to Notre Dame. Sure, it was stupid for a kid with that much talent not to alter course and get an education, but Jimmy kind of liked the stubbornness of Henry's decision. It reminded him of himself in arguments with Hazel — and similarly disappointing consequences.

So Henry had opportunity; there were witnesses galore to that, along with Henry's own admission. He said he had never worn the scarf found in his room, the one identical to that found in Larry's loft and the other found in the Izquierdo hall closet. The lab couldn't verify that. All three scarves looked new. Motive?

Henry shrugged. "He was an arrogant SOB. At first I was flattered by the attention, but that didn't last."

Oscar Wack was sure that the pogo stick was the key to the whole thing. What more did anyone need? Admittedly, it had been planted in Wack's room by Henry's accomplice, the previous suspect, but there it was.

"Where is what?"

Wack narrowed his eyes. "They were both tools of Izquierdo. He had enlisted them in his war against . . ." Wack worked his lips. "Against his colleagues."

"Oscar, don't be ridiculous." Lucy Goessen sat at the table in the Decio eatery with Jimmy and Wack.

"I am not in the habit of being ridiculous."

"All it takes is practice."

"Did they or did they not put Izquierdo's pogo stick in my office?"

"Oscar, even if they did, he did, whoever did, there is nothing sinister about it."

"Has anyone ever left a pogo stick in your office?"

"I wish they would."

Oscar sniffed. "Perhaps Raul bequeathed you his."

"I'll ask Pauline."

Jimmy asked Mrs. Izquierdo about it and she just looked at him.

"A pogo stick!" He began to describe it, and she stopped him. "I know what it is. Belonging to Raul?"

"For exercising?"

" 'Exercise is the simulated labor of the decadent.' I am quoting. One of his peeves was all the emphasis on healthiness. Wellness." She shuddered. "That I could sympathize with him on." She didn't have a spare pound on her, so she could afford to make light of exercise.

"Don't get me wrong. I run. It's all these machines, the factory look of the wellness center, that gets to me. Running is as ancient as cavemen."

"And cavewomen?"

Jimmy found himself responding to what he would have hesitated to call her flirtiness. Call it an irrepressible femininity. He hadn't felt this way since . . . Forget about it.

"So he didn't own a pogo stick?"

"Never."

Not to waste taxpayers' money, Jimmy mentioned it to Larry Douglas as something it would be nice to figure out. Larry got the message. Jimmy half expected him to lay a finger alongside his nose.

Jimmy himself sat in his office, staring at the wall. Someone had strangled Raul Izquierdo, and it looked as if Henry Grabowski would stand trial for it. By the time it got to court, the charge might have been whittled down to manslaughter; the jury would follow along, in their minds correcting procedures by reference to all the television dramas they had seen. The cops were the bums, the accused not only presumed innocent but all the more so because he had been accused. By the time it was over, Henry might be awarded a scholarship to Notre Dame.

Not funny.

Furlong had wangled a court appointment to defend Henry, who assured the lawyer he didn't have a dime.

"Justice isn't for sale."

"How much do they give you for representing me?"

Furlong ignored that. Jimmy left lawyer and client to their own devices. It was a dark thought that Fauxhall, the assistant prosecutor, had colluded in the appointment of Furlong. The little lawyer with the darting eyes could be the prosecution's secret weapon.

2

Philip Knight still talked with Jimmy about the case, but he thought his work was done.

"At least it wasn't a student," Father Carmody said. He was getting his cigar ready for the match. Holy Cross House was smoke free, but when reminded of it Carmody always replied, "All right. Where are the free smokes?" The nurses weren't likely to insist on the rule with someone who had the gravitas of Father Carmody. Roger's phrase. The lawlessness of gravity? Phil shook his head. He had to get away. The next thing you knew, he would be auditing classes.

"More snow is predicted," he told Father Carmody.

Father Carmody smiled. He liked a snow-bound campus. Notre Dame was the universe for the old priest, so he didn't feel deprived. His traveling days were over. Once he had spent a good portion of his time visiting various alumni around the country

— around the world, for that matter — and bringing home the bacon for Notre Dame. He didn't miss it as much as he claimed. In any case, alumni came to him. Quirk. Reminded of Quirk, Father Carmody lit his cigar and disappeared in a cloud of smoke.

"I'm surprised he hasn't moved back here. Like Bastable."

"Bastable."

So Phil got the story on Bastable. Roger had called Phil's attention to the op-ed page in the *Observer* that had recently appeared. After a few swipes at the publication in which he was appearing, Bastable settled into the persona of an Old Testament prophet. His was an open letter to the president. Recent events on campus were the beginning of a divine judgment on the university. Warnings. There was still time to turn back. That a professed atheist had been on the faculty of Notre Dame indicated the extent of the decline from the days of yore. Who knew what other horrible revelations might be made? And please don't be deluded into thinking that the resurrection of the Fighting Irish was a sign of divine approval. Whom God would destroy, he first makes mad. Fanatic.

Bastable spelled it out. Fans. It was pretty bad. Right there he lost whatever wild

266

sympathy he might have commanded. You don't talk that way about Notre Dame football. It didn't help that Bastable added that there are no atheists on the gridiron.

"You'd think he had been an English major," Father Carmody said.

What he was majoring in during his retirement years was divine discontent.

"Do you see much of him, Father?"

"I'm never in to cranks."

It was Roger's remark that he would like to meet Bastable that sent Phil to the town house overlooking the St. Joseph River. A large comfortable woman with her finger in a jumbo paperback, marking her place, answered the door. Phil told her who he was. She kept smiling. Then, stretching it a bit, Phil said Father Carmody had suggested he stop by.

"Carmody!"

She stepped aside, and the man who came forward was obviously Bastable.

"Philip Knight," the woman said, and slippered away.

Bastable's face lit up with delight. He had made the connection with Roger.

"Come in, come in." He took Phil's elbow and led him into what he called Command Central. He turned down the volume on Rush Limbaugh, then turned it off. "I'm taping it anyway. Why doesn't your brother ever return my calls?"

"This is quite a setup you've got here."

"State of the art. Where would we be without the Internet? At the mercy of the media, that's what. Take a pew, take a pew. Can I get you a drink?"

"No thanks."

"Diet Sprite. I drink six cans a day. It keeps the system running, if you know what I mean."

Phil was still standing, looking out at the river. "What a view."

Bastable stood beside him. "The awful thing is that I almost never notice it anymore."

When they finally sat, he told Phil of his plans for retirement. He and Florence would settle in South Bend, to be near the institutions that had formed them. "Florence is a St. Mary's girl." They had imagined taking part in campus events, attending lectures, plays, and of course sporting events.

"Who was it said you can't go home again? You can't go back to school again either. It's no longer there. But it isn't just that things are different. Tell me, what does your brother really think of Notre Dame?"

"We have an agreement. I don't speak for

him, and he doesn't speak for me."

"Okay. What do you think?"

"I came for the sports."

"Sure. That's fine. But you must have some view on where Notre Dame is headed."

"Mr. Bastable, you have to understand, I'm not Catholic. Roger is, but I'm not."

Bastable stared at him. "Not a Catholic? I'm surprised they didn't offer you a professorship."

"I'm a private detective."

Bastable moved forward in his chair. "I had heard that." He seemed to be thinking. "How would you like a job?"

"Not particularly. I'm more or less retired."

"I would make it worth your while."

Phil shrugged. He found he wanted to hear what Bastable had in mind.

"Look, it can be as hush-hush as you want. You're inside, you have connections. I think that atheist who was strangled was only the tip of the iceberg."

He wanted Phil to dig up dirt on Notre Dame. What kind of alumnus was he? Bastable seemed to sense the question.

"You know what our trouble is as alumni? We refuse to believe anything bad about this place. You don't graduate from Notre Dame.

At commencement you're turned into an alumnus. We trip over one another giving money to the place, and never ask what we are underwriting."

Phil heard him out. It was a shame that a man made himself as unhappy as Bastable clearly was. Maybe it was his way of being happy. Phil told him he wasn't interested.

"Think about it."

"I've met your classmate Quirk."

Bastable beamed. But then gloom returned. "He has some crazy scheme of getting Notre Dame to buy a villa in Sorrento. He actually wanted me to contribute." Bastable shook his head. "And he is pinning his hopes on Fred Fenster. Ha."

"You don't think Fenster will come through?"

"You know where he is right now? In a Trappist abbey in Kentucky. He thinks prayer is the answer."

"What's the question?"

"Maybe you're right," Bastable said enigmatically, and drank greedily from his can of Diet Sprite.

3

Larry Douglas felt that he was on His Majesty's Secret Service. He didn't tell Crenshaw that Jimmy Stewart had enlisted his help, and he didn't tell Laura either. She was as chummy as before, chummier, but Larry told her he wasn't sure he was completely over the flu.

"I need lots of rest."

"You shouldn't be working."

"Maybe not."

"I'll make soup and bring it over."

"I can't hold anything down," he lied.

Laura insisted that he go home immediately and get into bed. "I will explain to Crenshaw. Don't even answer the phone."

So Larry drooped and looked sick and got out of there. After hours on that damned bicycle it was good to get behind the wheel of his car. When he went through the campus entrance, he pulled in to Cedar Grove, got out his cell phone, and called the morgue.

"This is Larry," he said when Kimberley came on.

"I used to know someone by that name."

"I suppose you heard about Henry."

"Next they'll probably arrest your friend Laura."

"How would you like to do a little police work?"

"Like what?"

"I'll come by the morgue, okay?"

"We've got some free slabs."

It seemed a shame to be working for Jimmy Stewart and have no one know. He felt like a weasel, calling Kimberley with Henry under arrest, but after all Henry had grandly offered Kimberley to him on a platter. Have your old girl back. Henry was hard to like, no doubt about that, and Larry didn't know what he thought about the arrest. He remembered his own time downtown when he had been brought in by Jimmy and Phil Knight and there was Laura. He didn't like to remember how he had broken down and how Laura had comforted him. He stopped at his loft and changed and then went on to the morgue.

Feeley, the coroner, sat in his revolving chair, boxing the compass. He had been telling Kimberley for the hundredth time of his thwarted hopes for medical research, of the years at Mayo, of the bright future that had been dashed when he was told, run for coroner or your old man is on the street. If his father retired at sixty-five, Feeley still had years to go, and by then he'd be rusty, but he would try to get into Mayo's for a refresher. Why was he boring Kimberley with his sad story? Feeley was single and therefore, in theory at least, a rival, if Larry was in the running with Kimberley, that is.

"Business is dead," Feeley said sepulchrally when Larry asked if he could borrow Kimberley.

"Borrow me?"

" 'Neither a borrower nor a lender be.' "

Her eyes sparked; memories were enkindled. The way to her heart was through poetry.

"Let me use your phone book."

He turned to the yellow pages and looked up stores featuring athletic equipment, depressed to find so many. On the other hand, that meant a prolonged search.

"What are we after?"

"A pogo stick."

"Why not a unicycle?"

"We'll look at those, too."

The first half dozen stores said they didn't have pogo sticks in stock but they could order one for Larry. He told them maybe later, he would see if he could find a store that had one.

"I sold the only one I had two weeks ago."

"No kidding."

The clerk was adenoidal and had a bad case of acne. He couldn't keep his eyes off Kimberley.

"I sold it myself. To a real doll."

Larry had been about to get Kimberley out of there, but instinct told him to hold the phone. He asked the clerk to tell him about the customer and while he listened felt disappointment. He had been certain it would be Mrs. Izquierdo, but the woman the clerk was describing was more like Lucy Goessen.

"Did you get her name?"

"You want her name?"

"You don't have it?"

"I could look it up."

Larry flashed his Notre Dame security ID. The clerk looked at it and then at Larry, but he had seen enough television dramas to know about undercover cops. "Come on."

The back office made Larry's loft look neat. Sales slips were tossed into a shoe box for later filing.

"Kimberley can help you."

"What are we looking for?"

"Goessen."

"Watch your language."

"Lucy Goessen."

"That's who it was," the clerk cried. Then he found the slip.

"I'll take that."

"Oh, I can't let you do that."

There was a photocopying machine in a corner of the office. Larry suggested they make a copy of the sales slip.

"Please," Kimberley added, and the clerk flicked on the copier.

When they went out to the car, Larry felt that he had hit pay dirt. His first impulse was to go out to Decio and confront Professor Goessen with what he had learned. But what had he learned? That she had bought a pogo stick. He decided it would be better to report to Jimmy Stewart.

"Want to come along?" he asked Kimberley, when he had explained his decision.

"Then what?"

" 'Doubt that the stars are fire,' " he began, and she squeezed his arm.

4

In all outward respects, Lucille Goessen was a daughter of her time. In departmental meetings, she voted with her sisters as a block, on every ballot for college council, academic council, whatever, she voted for females as her grandmother had once voted for all the candidates with Irish names. On the matter of the *Monologues,* she did not question the department's sponsorship of the event, nor did she snicker at the rape warnings pasted all over the door of Hilda Faineant's door. "Fair warning," Raul had commented, but Lucy only smiled, not a breach of sisterly solidarity. But the outer was not the inner.

Lucy taught eighteenth- and nineteenth-century fiction. English majors professed to be taken by *Nightmare Abbey and Crotchet Castle,* which always turned out to be a bit of a pose. *Rasselas?* Forget it. Sometimes Lucy felt that she was feeding the disgust for literature that seemed departmental policy. It was Jane Austen who divided the sheep from the goats. The goats signed on to the dismissive stance of Kingsley Amis; the sheep knew they were in touch with something real. For the latter, step one was to rinse their minds of all the cinematic distortions of the divine Jane and get them to wallow in the text. In her heart of hearts, Lucy wanted a world where women were women and men were men, where courtship was a prolonged ritual, where love was forever, the good were rewarded and the evil punished. Henry had turned out to be one of the goats.

When Raul told her of the campus cop who was brighter than any student, Lucy was ready to dismiss it as typical Izquierdian hyperbole. It might even have been a new version of his line. But the mention of Goldsmith's *The Vicar of Wakefield* caught her attention.

"He's read it?"

"Several times. Not my sort of thing. You should talk with him."

"Send him over."

Henry had read a lot, no doubt about that, but it seemed somehow ammunition in a battle he was in. Even so, it was obviously a waste that he was in campus security. Why wasn't he a student?

"I can't afford it."

She kept her door open during his visit, as male professors had once prudently done with female students. Hilda cruised by a few times during the session, her manner disapproving.

Henry failed the Jane Austen test, and that was a shame. If he could stop thinking of literature as a weapon, he could have been interesting. But he was already a disciple of Raul Izquierdo's, alas. Worse, Henry reminded her of Alan.

In graduate school it had dawned on her that she had joined something like the nunnery. Maybe a vow of chastity wasn't in prospect, but neither was anything like an ordinary marriage. Lucy was on track to becoming a female academic, and everything else in her life was presumed to be secondary to that. A few dates convinced her that the males were interested in arrangements and little more. Isn't that what feminism meant? And then on a fateful cab ride to campus she met Alan. He was driving the cab. When they got there, he got out, opened the door for her, carried her luggage to her door. He refused a tip and noted the address, and she went inside liking it that he had liked her.

He called. They arranged to meet. She didn't want her housemates to know. From the start, she felt like Lady Chatterley about it. He was smart but uneducated. They bowled; they went to sports bars; she watched more games on television than she ever had in her life. And they never talked about the fact that she was a graduate student in English. She loved it. He became her reality principle. Then, in a whoosh of romantic impetuosity, after she had passed her written exams and needed respite, they became lovers.

"So, when will it be?"

"It?"

"The wedding."

He meant it. My God. "But I'm going to be a teacher."

"I have an aunt who's a teacher."

They got married. A civil ceremony. She moved in with him, not letting her friends know he was her husband. She was leading a double life. What would it be like if she dropped out of school and . . . And what? When she was with Alan that seemed possible, but then she was awarded a Fulbright to England. He just looked at her when she told him. She tried to explain to him what a coup that was, nobody got Fulbrights to England. It was the first time they really talked about her academic life. She tried to convince him they could go to Cambridge together. He kept on staring at her. So she had to decide. In her carrel in the library, she tried to convince herself that being the wife of a cabdriver was preferable to having an academic career, but she lost the argument. Only he wouldn't have been a cabdriver anymore. It seemed to be his argument to keep her. He said he planned to drive a semi on the interstates of the country.

What would Jane Austen have done? They didn't get a divorce, they just separated. Lucy went on her Fulbright, published several articles on Peacock, and was hired by Notre Dame. Confused hopes for the future began when Alan moved to South Bend. He could drive a cab anywhere. Raul came on to her relentlessly, but she managed to keep it all on the level of laughter. Until Pauline showed up at her office, hair to her shoulders, wearing a fingertip-length coat and a colorful scarf that hung to her ankles. She came in, shut the door, and asked what the hell was going on. Lucy had no idea what she was talking about.

"Raul. Don't think I don't know."

"Sit down. What do you know?"

How do you convince a wife that you

wouldn't take her husband if he came with the winning lottery ticket? In self-defense, she told Pauline about Alan. Like an idiot she wept while she told her story. Pauline sat looking at her with those beautiful big eyes that soon brimmed with tears. Then she told Lucy what it was like being married to Raul. Lucy felt a sisterly solidarity Hilda Faineant would not have understood. When Pauline got up to go, they embraced.

"What a scarf," Lucy said.

"I bought Raul one, too."

Of course Lucy didn't tell her about Raul's shenanigans with women students. She must know about that. But why had he invented an affair with a colleague to tease Pauline with? What a relief it had been to confide in Pauline about Alan.

Then weird things began to happen. There was the fire in Raul's wastebasket; his Corvette was firebombed. Lucy wondered if this was Oscar Wack's revenge. Oscar was the only colleague she had told about Alan. It was Oscar who brought up pogo sticks, saying wistfully that he'd had one when he was a kid. So she bought one for him, bringing it to campus early one morning and getting the cleaning lady to put it in Oscar's office. Surprise, surprise. Only the surprise had been on her.

For days after Raul's body was found, Lucy avoided the third floor of Decio. The memorial service for Raul was in the chapel in Malloy, and Pauline was tragically beautiful wearing a fedora, a black coat with a fur collar, and that many-colored scarf hanging to her knees like a defiant badge of grief.

"May his soul and the souls of all the faithful departed through the mercy of God rest in peace."

At which words, Pauline whispered to Lucy, "He had no soul."

5

The only English professor Mary Alice had ever liked was Lucy Goessen, and she had kept in touch with her, more or less, since switching majors. She had suggested doing a profile of Professor Goessen for *Via Media* but been dissuaded. "I don't have tenure."

Mary Alice understood. Any connection with the alternative paper could have been the kiss of death with Lucy's colleagues. Mary Alice did cover the memorial service for Professor Izquierdo and afterward talked with Lucy, waiting until she was finished commiserating with the strikingly beautiful Mrs. Izquierdo.

"Come to my office," Lucy said.

So they crossed over to Decio and took the elevator to the third floor. Before unlocking her door, Lucy stared at the closed door across the hall and shuddered. When they were settled with coffee, it was of Raul Izquierdo's death that they spoke.

"There are so many things about it that don't make sense."

"Well, they've arrested the man who did it."

"Yes." She took a deep breath. "So tell me what you've been doing."

Lucy seemed skeptical about her enthusiasm for Roger Knight, giving a little cry when she heard he was lecturing on F. Marion Crawford.

"Good grief."

"I know. But he can make anything interesting."

Lucy had never met Roger. Maybe that would have to wait until she had tenure, too. Mary Alice felt she was gushing when she explained what Roger's courses had meant for her. And she mentioned that Roger had been a private detective, with his brother Philip. Somewhat to her surprise, Lucy didn't express shock at this.

"I'd like to meet him."

"Oh, you should. I could set it up."

Lucy hesitated, then nodded. "Okay."

The following day, Mary Alice met Lucy in the library, and they walked through the parking lot east of the building to the village of graduate student houses where the Knights had an apartment.

Roger's size affected people in either of

two ways, but Lucy's reaction was one Mary Alice understood. It made you want to mother the massive Huneker Professor. After the introductions, Roger sank into his special chair and then, realizing his guests were still standing, started to rise. They stopped him.

"If only I had behaved in a more gentleman-like manner," he said.

"Mr. Darcy!" Lucy cried, and from then on the visit was a dream.

Listening to the chatter about Jane Austen, Mary Alice was aglow, having brought together two of her favorite professors to find that they were kindred spirits. Roger made popcorn and hot chocolate, falling snow was drifting by the windows, a Mozart piano concerto provided background music, it was wonderful. Inevitably, the conversation turned to the terrible events in Decio.

Roger said, "I know the detective in the case."

"Your brother?"

"Oh, Phil is just an auxiliary. I mean Jimmy Stewart."

Mary Alice described the memorial service and the beautiful Mrs. Izquierdo. "She was wearing the most colorful scarf. Long as a stole."

"I've met the young fellow who is accused

of the murder," Roger said. "Did you know him?"

"He was a protégé of Raul's. What on earth he is doing working in campus security I just don't understand."

"That is curious, about Mrs. Izquierdo's scarf."

"Oh, they each had one," Lucy said. "A matching set."

Roger thought about it. "Well, that explains two of them."

Philip Knight came in then, and Roger introduced him to Lucy, but Philip was preoccupied. He had just come from downtown.

"Anything new?"

"Henry Grabowski has confessed to killing Izquierdo."

6

After the women left, Roger asked Phil to tell him all about it.

"He says he did it."

"What led him to say that?"

"The widow showed up and asked to see him. Furlong put up a fuss, but Jimmy let them talk."

"What was the point of the visit?"

"She said she wanted to see the man who had killed her husband."

Ten minutes after Mrs. Izquierdo left, Henry asked to see Fauxhall, the assistant prosecutor, and confessed.

"Of course, Furlong will plead him not guilty, but Grafton the reporter was lurking around and he heard of it, so it will be public knowledge that the accused confessed to the crime."

"What does Jimmy think?"

Henry's confession cleared up all kinds of loose ends. He had access to Izquierdo's office; that had been known for some time. The protégé had become progressively disenchanted with his mentor, particularly his boasting about all the conquests he made with women students.

"Is that true?"

"Oscar Wack says his colleague was an animal."

"I suppose it could be established one way or another."

"I doubt that Jimmy wants to get into that."

"Of course not."

In any case, fed up with Izquierdo, Henry had decided to act. The fire in the wastebasket in Izquierdo's office suggested firebombing the Corvette.

"He admitted doing that?"

"He told them to check out his car." There were an empty gas can and lengths of rags in the trunk as Henry said there would be. He thought that would be a nice touch because of the threatening notes that Izquierdo had pasted together. Henry had delivered them, in his guise as campus security, all except the one to Oscar Wack. Izquierdo wanted to do that himself. It was Izquierdo's stoic reaction to the loss of his car that elevated Henry's efforts to a tragic level. The murder had been committed in the early evening. Henry was using Izquierdo's office; the professor showed up, chuckling about the fact that his jealous wife had refused him entry to his own house. Henry ceded the desk chair; Izquierdo sat, that long many-colored scarf around his neck. Henry stepped behind him, grasped the scarf, and used it to strangle Izquierdo.

"But no scarf was found at the scene."

"He says he took it with him. For a lark, he tossed it into Larry Douglas's loft, with the result that we all know."

"Until Mrs. Izquierdo came to the rescue. So much for the mystery of the three scarves."

Phil opened a beer and checked the TV listings but didn't turn on the set. "So that's that, I guess. I'll have to let Father Carmody know."

"I said it the first time," the old priest said, when Phil telephoned him. "Thank God it wasn't a student."

Phil nibbled at the remains of the popcorn and finished his beer.

Roger said, "You don't seem very happy."

"It's all so neat."

"Oh, I don't know. What about the pogo stick?"

"Larry Douglas looked into that. It seems it was bought by Professor Goessen."

"The woman who just left?"

"I suppose Jimmy will talk to her. But what's the problem? The thing was hers, not Izquierdo's. At least she bought it. Pauline Izquierdo just laughed at the suggestion that her husband would have exercised with such a thing."

It was the following day that Roger called Professor Goessen to ask her about the pogo stick. Her explanation removed any need to explain how it had got into Oscar Wack's office. Roger wasn't surprised when she confided in him about her estranged husband.

"What does it profit a woman if she gets tenure and suffers the loss of her husband?"

"Why can't I have both?"

Phil and Jimmy Stewart had begun to wonder, first separately, then together, about Pauline Izquierdo. It was her visit to Henry that preceded his confession that each of them found intriguing. Was it some kind of absurd gallantry, or had the sight of the widow brought on remorse?

"Gallantry?" Roger asked.

"The kid's a romantic. He reads poetry."

"Ah."

But Roger was thinking of what Henry had confided in him about his unsuccessful seduction of Mrs. Izquierdo, prompted by her husband. When Phil and Jimmy went off to a Notre Dame hockey game, Roger called a cab. He had to have a talk with Henry.

Half an hour later, a cab pulled up in front of the building and Roger, all bundled up, moved slowly out to it. The driver hopped out and came to help him.

"Thank you, thank you. Do you think I'll fit?"

The cabbie laughed. "You should see the size of some of my passengers."

With an effort, and the help of the driver, Roger was wedged into the backseat, and they set off.

"The jail?"

Then Roger noticed the license displayed over the rearview mirror. Alan Goessen. His eyes met the driver's in the mirror.

"I'm going to visit a murderer."

"The kid who killed the professor?"

"That's his story."

"He performed a public service." They stopped for a red light. Alan said, "You know, I met the guy, the professor. What a jerk."

"How so?"

"I knew guys like him in the service. Real Don Juans, all they talked about was their conquests. Most of them fantasies."

"Where did you meet him?"

"He was sitting right where you are. I drove him home from the airport one night."

Roger remembered Lucy's story of how Pauline had come to her, accusing her of dallying with Raul. Hell hath no fury? But then came another thought.

"I know your wife, Alan. She's a brilliant woman."

The light changed, and the cab moved forward. Alan was avoiding the rearview mirror.

"Did Izquierdo talk about Lucy?"

The cab seemed to slow, then regained speed. "What do you mean?"

"She was one of his imaginary conquests."

"The guy was a jerk."

"There seems to be a consensus on that."

"His wife was no better."

"Oh."

"Driving a cab is like being a cop, you see the seamy side of everything. She was having an affair with that kid. I know, I drove him there."

"The night he killed the husband."

Alan hesitated. "You're right."

The rest of the drive was mostly in silence.

At the courthouse, Alan helped Roger out

of the cab, then took his elbow and walked him to the entrance.

"Could you come back for me?"

"Sure."

"In an hour?"

Alan gave him a little salute, and Roger pushed through the revolving door.

"I'm Philip Knight's brother," Roger told the corpulent desk sergeant, who, looking at the massive speaker, seemed to grow thinner.

"So what?"

Roger sought and found his identification as a private investigator.

"I suppose it's all right."

"Think of him as a client."

"Is he?"

"You can ask him."

The sergeant thought about that, then decided against the effort it would take. He made arrangements for Henry to be brought to a visiting room and had an officer show Roger to it.

Roger was settled somewhat precariously on a chair when Henry was led in. He stared at Roger, then smiled. "What brings you here?"

" 'When I was in prison you visited me.' "

"Sure." Henry sat across from Roger.

"So you murdered Raul Izquierdo?"

Henry just looked at him.

"Someone confesses to a crime either because he did it or because he is trying to protect someone else."

"Does that exhaust the possibilities?"

"They are the only ones we need. So you think Pauline murdered her husband?"

"Look, I did it, and that's that."

Roger shook his head. "But you couldn't have."

Henry smiled. "Did implies could."

"An unassailable principle, whose counterpart is: could not have, therefore did not. I refer to the second scarf, the one you say you put in Larry Douglas's loft."

Henry hunched forward. He was enjoying this as a puzzle. Roger could imagine the sessions Henry had had with Izquierdo.

"Why not?"

"Pauline put it there."

"Why would she do a thing like that?"

"The question is rather why you would have. You had no reason to throw suspicion on Larry Douglas. He was a friend of yours. The fact that you did not come forward when that scarf was found in Larry's place proves that you knew who did it."

"That's pretty flimsy."

"The truth is never flimsy. Of course, the scarf is relatively unimportant. More important is your alibi."

"What alibi?"

"I understand it is a delicate matter. You described your seduction of Pauline Izquierdo as unsuccessful. But it wasn't, was it? She is your alibi."

"That's crazy."

"And you are hers, aren't you? When did you leave her that night?"

Henry sat back. "You've been reading too many novels. That's a plot worthy of F. Marion Crawford."

"Indeed it is. You would confess, there would be a trial, and she would come to your rescue and say that you were with her at the time of the murder. That's the plan, isn't it?"

Henry smiled. "It's your story."

Roger put his hands flat on the table. "And Izquierdo was already dead when you had your rendezvous with Pauline."

Clearly this had not occurred to Henry. Roger recalled for him the supposed time of the murder. "That was before you went to her, wasn't it?"

"Oh, come on." But there was a speculative look in Henry's eye.

"So you see, you can't be alibis for one another." Roger paused. "Something I am sure Pauline realizes."

Henry now had a realization of his own. He avoided Roger's eyes as if he were reviewing the events of the night Raul Izquierdo was strangled.

"She wouldn't do that to me!"

"Let's go back to your F. Marion Crawford plot. You think she killed her husband, she thinks you did. Which of you suggested your confessing? Of course, it could have been either of you who confessed, but noblesse oblige. You confess, the charade begins, she testifies, and the upshot is you are both exonerated. That was the idea, wasn't it? But why should she exonerate you if she did it?"

Henry pushed back from the table. "Save this kind of crap for your students."

"Do you trust her that much?"

Henry stood up, and the door of the room opened. An officer looked in. "Your cab is here."

"Would you have him come in here?"

"The driver?"

"Please."

"You through with him?" He meant Henry.

"Not yet."

Then Alan Goessen was standing in the doorway. He looked at Henry and Henry looked at him.

"Hi, kid."

Henry said, "Who is this?"

"Your real alibi, Henry. I regret to say that this is the man who murdered Raul Izquierdo."

POSTSCRIPT

There were some who expressed surprise at the way Alan Goessen had reacted to Roger's accusation, but Roger was not among them. It is for the Izquierdos of this world, and their apprentices such as poor Henry Grabowski, to so blind the eye of conscience that evil may parade as good. Alan's fundamental decency rendered him helpless before the truth of what he had done.

He did wheel and leave the room, and he might have left police headquarters if Phil and Jimmy Stewart had not arrived. An indication from Roger sufficed for them to prevent Alan's going, and then, feeling surrounded, almost with relief, he acknowledged the truth of what Roger had said.

Ahead lay the slow turning of the wheels of justice. Roger found that he felt sorrier for Lucy than he did for her husband. There must be some elemental sense of the rightness in killing a man who had wronged one's wife. The irony was that, whatever the truth of Raul Izquierdo's claim to be the playboy of the western world, South Bend division, there had been nothing between him and Lucy. When the truth of this was brought home to Alan, he looked at his estranged wife with an indescribable expression. She took him in her arms, and in a broken voice he asked her forgiveness. When a plea of innocence was entered for him, it seemed to have some plausibility.

"He'll probably walk," Jimmy Stewart said. He didn't sound regretful.

Larry Douglas had been accused, and he was free. Henry Grabowski had been accused, and he was free. The two young men were not true precedents for Alan Goessen, but who knew what might happen in the present state of the courts?

The liberated Henry had been reunited with Kimberley, whose mind now seemed adequate enough to match her beauty. Larry Douglas stopped by with a possessive Laura clinging to his arm, her unmittened hand displaying a diamond.

"Congratulations!" Roger said, but it was Laura who said thank you.

ABOUT THE AUTHOR

Ralph McInerny is the author of more than thirty books, including the popular Father Dowling mystery series, and has taught for more than fifty years at the University of Notre Dame, where he is the director of the Jacques Maritain Center. He has been awarded the Bouchercon Lifetime Achievement Award and was recently appointed to the President's Committee on the Arts and Humanities. He lives in South Bend, Indiana.

The employees of Thorndike Press hope you have enjoyed this Large Print book. All our Thorndike and Wheeler Large Print titles are designed for easy reading, and all our books are made to last. Other Thorndike Press Large Print books are available at your library, through selected bookstores, or directly from us.

For information about titles, please call:
(800) 223-1244

or visit our Web site at:
www.gale.com/thorndike
www.gale.com/wheeler

To share your comments, please write:
Publisher
Thorndike Press
295 Kennedy Memorial Drive
Waterville, ME 04901